Happy Disenchantment Day

Short Stories of Hapless Holidays

Bunbury Writers Group

Dedicated to all the people of the world
whose good intentions turn to disaster.

"When disaster strikes, it tears the curtain away from the festering problems that we have beneath them."
President (then Senator) Barack Obama

*"If you can meet with Triumph and Disaster
And treat those two impostors just the same."*
Rudyard Kipling.

*The Bunbury Writers Group
would like to acknowledge the past, present and future
Wardandi Noongar people as the first storytellers on our
homeland, Bunbury.*

*We are grateful that we are able to meet and write stories
from this place.*

Contents

Preface

As we get older, holidays—and by that, we mean days of cultural celebration or observance—lose the shininess that they had when we were children.

We remember the anticipatory belly-jiggling of the night before Christmas, Easter, and our birthdays with keen fondness. It was a time of magic. The lead up to [insert said day] felt different, special. How can we explain it better? It was as if the air smelt sweeter, the colours were brighter, and the days were longer.

Perhaps, it's the magic of childhood—the sorcery of special days that fade and pale over time as we age. Our memories remain shiny.

Perhaps, it's because as adults, we know the hard work that goes into making these days feel special to our children and loved ones. We try to recreate the magic we felt in childhood, the magic that becomes the familial tradition we see as our legacy. Afterall, kids don't see the days of cleaning and cooking that come before a celebration! They don't understand why we only see 'those' relatives once a year, they don't understand the grimaces disguised as smiles. They certainly do not understand the trap of capitalist commercialisation.

For adults, these days *can* be of celebration. Still, they can also be days of disenchantment—something we must get through because society expects it of us. In this book, we have taken this feeling and used it as our guiding light, writing about how these days have gone awry, ended disastrously, or in an unseen twist.

'*Happy Disenchantment Day*' is a collection of adult short fiction dedicated to these celebratory days.

From postmodern Christmas and Easter, to days that deliver more bangs than fireworks. At the same time, we see the heartbreak of loss of those things important to us.

Valentine's Day isn't always a day of roses and romance, or if it is, perhaps it is fleeting or explosive. Halloween can be scary and life-threatening, whereas patriotic days are not what you'd expect.

So, make a cup of tea (or get a wine) and settle back and join our storytellers as we raise our glasses and toast to:

'Happy Disenchantment Day'.

Lee Harsen
Bunbury Writers Group

Bunbury Writers Group would like to acknowledge
The City of Bunbury
for the arts grant we were recently awarded.
Part of the grant allowed us a collective space in which this
book was created.

Lost Things

It's all going to plan, until the lost teddy. Maddy rages in the back of the car, whilst I keep my eyes on the road. I tighten my grip on the steering wheel and count to five, trying to slow my increasing heart rate.

In between frantic sobs, she pleads, 'Please, can we go back, Mum? We have to find Rosie.'

I shake my head. 'Maddy, I told you to leave her at home. If she was that special, you wouldn't have left her behind. We don't have time to go back.'

I know Maddy won't accept this response. I know she won't be rational about this. But I find it hard to be sympathetic today. It's Christmas Eve and I have a list of jobs as long as Maddy's ability to whine. Rosie could be anywhere. I anticipate that the rest of the car ride will be traumatic and expect a headache by the time I pull into the driveway. My ears ring as Maddy's voice increases in pitch.

'Turn the car around! Someone might take her. Let's go back… please.'

'Look, Maddy, we can't go back now. We've got family coming around tomorrow and I have so many things to do still. Maybe we can come back another day.'

Maddy's hope is crushed and she lets it out in an anguished wail. She kicks the back of the chair.

'You're so mean! If I lost you, I wouldn't go back and look

for you. This is the worst Christmas Eve, ever.'

Considering she's only had seven Christmas Eves, my eyes roll at her dramatics.

The rest of the day goes as I expect. She mopes around while I hurry about the house getting last minute cooking and cleaning finished. Her mood picks up when we settle in to watch a Christmas movie and I think perhaps she has forgotten. But when I tuck her in, she sighs and asks, 'Do you think Rosie will be safe, wherever she is?'

I feel a pang of guilt for my harshness earlier that day and berate myself for letting my stress get in the way. I'm calmer now and I use this time to make it up to her.

I brush her hair away from her eyes and keep my hand on her forehead. 'Honey, I'm sure she is.' I pause, torn between putting a chink in her childhood innocence or preparing her for the many disappointments in life. I settle for somewhere in between. 'But you loved her when she was with you and if she stays lost you know you made her little teddy heart happy while she was here. You gave her lots of cuddles and kept her warm at night and had lots of tea parties. We can look for her tomorrow, but if we don't find her, remember that sometimes, things stay lost. But the memories are with us forever.'

Maddy looks at me with her wide eyes and whispers, 'Like when Daddy stayed lost. Rosie helped me when I was missing him. I just feel sad that Rosie might be alone.'

My heart breaks just a little more at the mention of her Dad and I try to push the pain down, so I can say the right thing.

'Baby girl, you've got such a big, caring heart. Please try to not worry. I promise, after we have our Christmas lunch, we'll go back and look for her. Until then, be excited about Santa coming and opening presents tomorrow.'

Maddy yawns and turns on her side. I tuck her in and blow

her a kiss as I walk out the door. I'm in the hallway when she calls out, 'I didn't mean what I said before. If I lost you, I wouldn't stop until I found you.'

'Darling girl, me too. I love you, Maddy.' My voice breaks; I swallow, straighten my back and go get her present ready to put under the tree.

*

I'm packing the dishwasher and trying not to think about the mess I have to clean, when Maddy skips up to me. 'Lunch is over and everybody's gone; can we go look for Rosie now?'

I survey the kitchen, scan my eyes over the crumpled napkins, leftover food on plates and ripped bon bons that litter the table. Going on a teddy hunt is the last thing I feel like doing but I remember the promise I made. I grab the keys.

'You ready to go on a Christmas rescue mission?'

Maddy jumps and giggles; the glimmer of hope makes her eyes sparkle. I am impressed, and a little envious, at how easy it is for her to remain hopeful when the odds are against her.

*

We've spent the last hour and a half re-tracing our steps and still, Rosie remains lost. I have given up and grown impatient, but Maddy insists we keep trying.

'Maddy, we've tried our best. We can't stay out here all day. Don't you want to go home and play with your presents?' I try some reverse psychology but she's smarter than that. As frustrating as it is, I wish I had even half of her determination. 'Look, we'll go for another half an hour. If she doesn't turn up, we'll just have to accept she's gone.'

Maddy folds her arms and purses her lips. We continue to walk the path we took yesterday, searching for a flash of the rainbow bow tie that Rosie has tied around her neck.

3

I'm just about to open my mouth to call it, when I hear footsteps behind us. I turn around to see a dishevelled man coming towards us. Instinctively, I pull Maddy closer to me and keep walking.

'Excuse me,' he calls. 'Are you looking for something?'

His appearance unnerves me and I consider ignoring him. But we are out in the open and I'm not one to be rude.

'My daughter lost her teddy yesterday. We're looking for it.'

Maddy smiles at him, despite his unkempt hair and knotty beard.

'Well, Merry Christmas. I think this may be yours.'

He pulls Rosie out of his baggy jacket and extends his arm towards Maddy. She squeals in delight and my mouth gapes open. She takes the teddy from his outstretched arm and hugs it close.

'I saw you drop it yesterday, but you were getting into your car and didn't hear me call out.'

'Thank you so much. Maddy's been beside herself. I can't believe you happened to be here again today.'

'I don't live far away. Just over there, actually.' He turns and points to a bus shelter, where a sleeping bag and trolley have claimed the space.

'Oh,' I say awkwardly.

Maddy gives the man another beaming smile. 'Thank you for looking after Rosie. I knew I'd find her!'

He bends down so he can get to Maddy's eye level. I try not to scrunch my nose up.

'It was my pleasure. It gets a bit lonely at Christmas so she was a good companion.'

Maddy clings tighter to Rosie and nods her head. 'She is. Before Daddy left, he gave me Rosie. Since then, we've always been together.'

'I knew there was something special about her. I'm glad I could bring her back to you.'

'Thanks again,' I say. 'You've just made Maddy's Christmas. Turned a disaster into a miracle.'

'Glad to help. It felt good to be useful.' He looks to Maddy again. 'Now, enjoy the rest of your Christmas and have fun playing with Rosie.' He begins to walk away and Maddy watches him leave.

'Isn't it wonderful that we found Rosie? Now let's go home.' I reach for Maddy's hand but she starts to run towards the man.

'Wait!' Maddy calls. She puts Rosie in the man's hands. He takes the teddy with a question in his eyes. 'Rosie wasn't lost. She just found someone new. Merry Christmas.'

The man brings the teddy to his chest. He looks at my daughter with complete gratitude.

'But you love her so much. Are you sure?'

She nods her head. 'I think you need her more than I do. And now I know where she is, I won't be worried anymore.'

He looks at us both. 'Thank you. Thank you so much. This is the best Christmas I've had in a long time.'

I take Maddy's hand and blink the tears away. 'What you just did, Maddy. Wow. That was so kind.'

She skips back to the car. 'Memories are with us forever. Isn't that right, Mum?'

Suzi Faed

Terra Nullius

I was born on the 26th of January. Australia Day. Bonzer having your birthday on a day when everyone's off work, eating snags and going to the beach. When I was a kid, I was convinced the fireworks were for me. We used to head down to the foreshore, Mum driving cos Dad had already had a skinful, and we'd yell and cheer, and Mum would do my birthday cake at the end of the show. I'd blow out the candles in the night air, and all the other families with their picnics would join in singing me *Happy Birthday*.

This year is a special one. It's my eighteenth. Mum kisses me as I come into the kitchen and I pull away, but she's having none of it, giving me a hug as tight as she can, and I don't mind really. Dad's already out on the patio firing up the barbie and yelling at me to come out and have my first legal beer with him. But it's not even nine, and I want to drive over to Jeannie's so she can join us. We've been dating for two years now. High school sweethearts.

There's something about Jeannie… which sounds like a song, '*She keeps me coming back for more. Oh yeah.*'

I strum air guitar and wish I could sing in tune. Her Mum and Dad are pretty liberal too; they let me stay over. My Mum turns a blind eye and kisses her rosary beads for me. I'm not sure if she's worried for my soul or praying we don't get knocked up. I wouldn't mind if Jeannie did get caught. I'm going to ask her to marry me when I finish my apprenticeship, just six months to go now.

Dad's insistent though, so I knock one back and let the old man give me a hug. No sage advice, but I do get a Woollies sausage in a bun with plenty of onions and tomato sauce, just the way I like them. I shout thanks in between mouthfuls and with half still in my hand I duck out before the whole house is up, and the neighbours pile in and I can't getaway.

Jeannie is ready for me when I get to hers. She looks fit in her shorts and bikini top and her parents have wrapped me a gift. I unwrap it awkwardly, saying thank you over and over, and like you shouldn't have and all that, while they smile, eyes watching me, glad that they have. It's a tankard engraved with 'Happy Eighteenth Mike lots of love the Lyndhurst family'. With three x's underneath representing kisses. Melody, Jeannie's mum says, 'To remember the day. Happy Birthday, Micky, can't believe that you are all grown up, be our Jeannie's turn next.'

I say thanks again and she gives me a hug, and Rod, Jeannie's dad shakes my hand. I can't stand all the fuss. I place my hand into Jeannie's gripping tightly, she smiles at me, and I invite them to come around to my parents for the barbie. I know they won't.

Pulling away, with the windows down full, to get the breeze, I'm feeling like I've won a million bucks. Jeannie sits beside me, her hand resting in my lap. She says that she has something for me too but she's going to save it for later when we are alone. As we pull up on the grass outside the house, my mates have already arrived, and before too long, I'm a few beers and burgers into my birthday. Jeannie wants to go to my room, but I've had a few now and I'm doing the Macarena with Auntie Sue and getting it on a bit with Maria, the pretty Italian brunette. I can see that Jeannie is looking mad, but the beer is making me feel brave, and I still dare to give her a kiss. She looks at me, her grey eyes getting steely, her bottom lip tucked under. She grabs my hand and I let her lead me into my bedroom. We both drop on the bed and I roll on top of her, kissing her mouth. She turns her head away.

'Micky, stop a minute I want to give you your present.'

I tell her she is my present, pinning her down to the bed, knowing I'm much stronger. She tries to wriggle free. The more she wriggles, the tighter I hold her.

'Micky stop your hurting me.'

I come to my senses, let her go, look at her wrists, red and sore.

'Fuck Jeannie, I'm sorry… hey what's my present?'

She circles her wrist with her other hand. I pull it up to my mouth. Kissing it better.

She pulls it away. 'You don't deserve a present'.

I pull my most loveable face, knowing she will give in. She puts her hand into her pocket and pulls out a small box and hands it to me.

Inside is a cygnet ring. Just the right size for my little finger. Inside is engraved, 'Love U forever'

I put it on my finger. Pull her close and kiss her long.

Next time it will be me putting a ring on her finger. She'll be mine forever.

We lie back down on the bed. Jeannie sleeps, her head on my chest, the smell of apple shampoo waking my body up. I want to roll her over, wake her up, undo her bikini top, but I am also entranced by the sound of her breathing, so I let her be. Instead, I listen to the party, to my Aunties laughter getting louder and Dad getting insistent with anyone that tries to leave that they need to stay for one more.

The room is getting hotter, and Jeannie's hair is damp on my chest. I roll her over and get up. Shower and change. When

I return to the bedroom, she's awake, and it's already getting dark outside. We head back to the party, to the clamour of noisy aunts and drunk uncles who leer at Jeannie and me, with a, 'we know what you've been doing' look. A few of my mates are still knocking back beers, everyone's been drinking since ten; some of them have drunk themselves sober. My Mum's fussing around making more food. My Dad is playing party tunes and dancing with the next-door neighbour.

'We are going to head down to see the fireworks,' I say to anyone who's listening.

I'm pretty much ignored. It might be my birthday but everyone else has moved on. Except for my Mum of course, who says, 'What about the cake?'

'Save it, Mum, they are all too far gone to enjoy it.'

She smiles at me, and for the first time, I notice that her eyes don't smile at the same time. I notice she looks weary.

A couple of my mates, pile into the back of the ute. We're only ten minutes from the foreshore. Jeannie is quiet. Still looking at her bloody wrists. I take her hand and kiss it. She wants to go home and change. So, we stop off at hers first. I knock back a beer, while we wait. We start to sing in loud voices 'Why are we waiting?' I see Melody look out the window; she waves, and I wave back. I hope Jeannie ends up like her Mum. Unlike mine, she still dresses young, and I reckon she'd be up for a bit of fun. Smitty, my mate, wolf whistles at her and waves too. She looks embarrassed, but pleased.

'Finally, Jeannie,' I mouth as she comes out of the house. She's changed into a sweater and jeans. But she's one of those girls that would look good in a sack.

When we get to the foreshore, we all sit in the back of my Ute, beers in hand, waiting for the fireworks. Jeannie pulls out a bottle of wine from her bag and starts necking it. Smitty has other plans though, bringing music and weed, he winks and shouts, 'LET THE PARTY BEGIN!'

The music has a deep bass beat and other cars pull up around ours. People I know begin to get out. A lot of them are already pretty drunk or high.

Smitty says, 'Couldn't let your birthday pass without a proper party mate.'

He man-hugs me and hands me a pill. I swig it down with the beer.

It's all getting a bit messy and I can see some families staring at us – we are behaving like louts – and they pick up their picnics, turn their kids away, giving us filthy looks and head further up the foreshore away from us. I look around for Jeannie, but I can't see her. The fireworks begin and their light illuminates the ground. Jeannie is just up ahead. Some guy has his arm around her. I am going to fucking kill him. She's unsteady on her feet and he's trying to hold her up, but I don't care. No one touches her. Australia Day, my eighteenth birthday, the first time I hit Jeannie.

Louise Tarrier

The Second Coming

Marly perched on the edge of the bathtub and, using her compact mirror for a surface, cut a gram of coke into six little lines using the Amex card she'd lifted from a bar earlier in the evening. From downstairs, a deep bass pounded up through the cracked lino floor, seeped through the walls and thumped in Marly's head. She swayed with the beat, the drugs she'd been consuming throughout the evening loosening her limbs and her inhibitions.

The place, she had no clue who owned it, was a shithole and the bathroom, one of a few, was as bad as the rest. The walls had probably been white, once upon a time, but had endured years of sun bleaching, crack smoke and vomit, so were now the sort of yellow you'd mostly associate with soaked-in dried-up piss stains on a mattress. The flooring, freezing under Marly's bare feet, was brown lino tiles with deep cracks and missing pieces. She idly found herself wondering why the owner had gone with a brown floor, only to install muted-blue plastics for the sink and the tub. She wondered if maybe the blue was an effort to disguise the stains gained from the type of depravities that had gone on in here over the years.

Sliding as carefully as she could from the tub onto the cold tiles, her reflected coke balanced like a treasured possession, Marly was searching for the rolled up twenty in her purse when a shadow appeared behind her.

'I would probably hold off on the blow, in your condition,' a gravelly voice said. Not spoken as a suggestion, but an order.

Marly spun, ready to spring up, scratch the prick's eyes out, but when she saw him – how beautiful he was – she paused momentarily, and instead said, 'In my what?'

The man wasn't anyone she recognised from the party downstairs, although three straight days on pills and coke probably wouldn't help in that department anyway. He was well over six-foot and had a wave of thick dark hair, only slightly grey at the temples. He had a few days' worth of stubble on his angular jawline, and he fucking *glowed*. His eyes were the deep blue of oceans, sharp and intelligent, and Marly thought she wouldn't mind a bit of whatever he was on.

He knelt in front of her and took her hand. Her usual instinct, to pull away and punch him in the throat, was completely undone. He was magnetic. She couldn't have moved, even if she'd wanted to. 'Your condition. You're… pregnant. With child. Knocked up. However you want to phrase it.' His shrug nonchalant, his smile amused.

Marly laughed and managed to let go his hand, sliding on her backside to the far wall. 'Firstly, no I'm not, and secondly, who the holy shit are you to tell me that I am?'

Standing and straightening out his beyond crumpled Black Sabbath tee-shirt , the man raised his hands in mock defence. 'Firstly, yes you are, and secondly, I'm Gabe. I'm a… messenger, shall we say? Actually, and not wanting to toot my own horn here, but I'm more like *The* Messenger.'

If he wasn't so bloody spectacular to look at, Marly would've gotten up and stomped out, coke forgotten. It's not like there wasn't plenty more where it came from. But something kept her on the ground, only able to look up at the stranger and laugh nervously.

She finally mustered, 'Fuck you, Gabe.'

'Sure,' he said, gazing down at her. 'But more pressing is the issue of the child.' He turned away and checked his reflection in the wall mirror. Running a hand through his hair, which seemed to ripple and shine, he smiled at what he saw. Then he sat gently on the toilet lid and clasped his hands together, expectantly looking at Marly.

Twenty-three years old, Marly was still as stubborn and sullen as a teenager. She found the twenty in her purse and snorted the fattest line of the six. Taking it deep, she allowed her eyes to close and waited for the hot sensation to work its way down her throat and into her blood stream; she never bored of the rush, the dizzying sensation behind the eyes as the drug dominated her body and softened the edges of her reality. Rolling her shoulders, she was back in the room. Blue eyes snapped open, fixed on Gabe, her pupils huge. 'Want one, Gabe?' She proffered the compact mirror and the twenty.

'Not sure the boss would approve,' he replied smiling, 'but how about this. We share some blow, and you hear me out about this baby.'

'There is no baby. But sure, Gabe, whatever you say.'

Pulling the compact across the tiles, Gabe knelt and thoroughly enjoyed a couple of lines, before saying, 'There definitel—'

The bathroom door opened with a crash, the bass from below, all but faded into the background before, filled the room, making it small. Marly jumped to her feet and was on the drunken intruder in a second, grabbing the front of his shirt, pushing him into the hallway, shouting in his face, 'What the fuck? Get out!'

'Just need to piss, man,' the guy slurred, his eyes wide but unfocused, he cowered back from the enraged Marly.

'So use the garden like everyone else, we're busy.'

She pushed him onto the landing then spun and slammed

the door closed behind her, turning the lock even though its functionality seemed minimal, given that it was barely attached to the door, the underlying wood was mouldy and rotten.

'You're very angry,' Gabe said calmly. He hadn't so much as twitched at the interruption.

'Must be all those pregnancy hormones,' Marly shot back. She didn't sit – she couldn't now, she was pumped – instead she paced back and forth to the bathtub, counting her steps, counting the tiles, but neither in order. Numbers were dancing in her head and she was enjoying the freedom of their randomness. Why did it have to be 1, 2 3, anyway? Who said? Why couldn't it be 7, 2, 1? Imagine that…

The whirl in her head stopped abruptly as Gabe said matter-of-factly, 'Your pregnancy is advanced, and this baby will be here soon, and he's going to save you. In fact, he might just save all of us.'

Marly stopped her pacing. 'Oh please. I don't need saving. Rehab, maybe, but I'm all good.'

In a blink Gabe was beside her, standing so close that Marly could feel his breath on her hair. He cupped his hands in front of him, turned towards her, and whispered, 'May I?'

Without waiting for a response, he pushed his hands firmly against her stomach. This time she didn't wait, she pulled back a loosely balled fist and delivered a blow into his chest.

'What the hell?'

Gabe laughed and stumbled backwards. 'You felt him, didn't you? I did.'

'I felt nothing,' Marly said.

'His name will be James, and he will be part of you, because you've been chosen, for whatever reason, and he will also be part of Him. He will be delivered by me, and he will have his own Kingdom, his own palace.'

'Him?' Marly's balled fists dropped by her side and she

stepped back towards Gabe, her hands loose and shaking, either from too much blow or fear of the faint but firm thuds she had felt in her belly, responding to Gabe's touch.

'Him,' Gabe confirmed.

'I've just been checked. I've got nothing, no diseases, no infections. Definitely no baby. I'm always safe,' Marly insisted, but she stepped even closer to Gabe, The Messenger, better wanting to understand, feeling that closing the distance between them would help.

'This is a child given to you by Him, and he's a Spirit. This isn't some 10-minute-back-seat hook up. And you are ready for this,' Gabe's tone was so sure. He closed the remaining gap between them and took Marly's hands.

'Am I tripping? I'm tripping. This is that LSD,' she whispered.

'No.'

'I need more coke.'

Gabe clicked his fingers. The compact mirror, the left-over powder and the rolled up twenty disappeared from the room. 'You need to leave with me now. We need to prepare.'

'Prepare? For… the baby. James?' The foreign words tumbled from Marly's mouth slowly, a stark contrast to the terrifying rate at which her heart was beating.

'Yes. You need to sleep, and then to eat, and then to get better.'

Marly nodded and gathered her bag from the floor. She stepped in front of the wall mirror and tilted her head at her reflection. She felt like she'd never seen the person looking back at her before. The dark circles which had been a feature under her eyes for the last five years were gone; her cheekbones were still protruding a little too harshly, but a rose coloured blush sat high on them, and her eyes, even with their massive coke-blown pupils, were alert. Ready.

'I've never been this high,' she murmured to herself, whilst staring at Gabe in the mirror.

'Don't be afraid,' he whispered, suddenly right at her shoulder, pulsating with a golden hue, a visible energy.

Marly *was* afraid. 'Where are we going?'

Gabe considered this for a moment as he took Marly's hand and led her to the weakly-locked door. Downstairs they made their way through the thrum of dancing strangers and writhing bodies, and with a Devil's grin, Gabe said, 'We need to find a stable.'

Nina Peck

Hearts and Souls

The smell of roses mingles with desperation and filters upwards from the market. Humans scurry from chocolate stand to floral vendor, to stalls selling home-made cards, purchasing professed devotion crafted by another's hand.

Amora scrunches her nose as she judges them, her cherubian features morphing into something more calculated. She strokes the length of an arrow, twirling it like a baton between long, pale fingers, studying the mortals with her black eyes.

Hunting.

There's a sweaty man in a grey suit who stops in front of a flower stall. He grabs the first bouquet he sees, a bunch of Chrysanthemums.

Amora scoffs, incredulous that after centuries of horticulture, many humans haven't bothered to learn the meanings of flowers before purchasing them and thrusting them at the ones they claim to love. Unless his spouse is laying six feet deep in a cemetery, the ridiculous fool is about to deliver a very mixed message to his partner. However, Amora reasons, his significant other is probably just as oblivious, so what does it matter?

The man jogs away and Amora huffs out a frustrated breath. She twirls her wrist in a delicate movement and a tablet appears in her palm. Thousands of messages flash on the screen and she uses her index finger to focus into her current location. There are more than usual, which is to be expected, but annoyance flares in her chest anyway. So many entitled people have begged to find The One, as if the experience of true love is a once in a lifetime opportunity and limited to one per person.

That's the problem with humans, Amora thinks as she hovers closer to the crowd. They're small minded and shallow, unable to see past their two-kilometre Tinder radius.

She's still scrolling, eyes locked on to the screen, as she reaches the ground. The gentle movement of her wings causes a light breeze. The humans ignore it, or don't notice, blissfully unaware of Amora's descent into their midst. Unseen, she glides through the throngs of people as they flit like drugged up butterflies from one stall to another.

She's passed a dozen potential couples and a small voice reminds her that she should have moved on to the next location by now. But, for all her contempt, Amora is picky in her role. Love isn't something you hand to just anybody. These days it's getting harder to find humans worthy of such a responsibility, especially today.

Do they not realise that there are 364 other perfectly wonderful days to fall in love, to be in love, to give love? The idea of a sole day dedicated to an emotion which should be given freely and without expectation leaves a bad taste in Amora's mouth, and every year she decides she's going to quit... but the prospect of a world without love is scarier than a world that takes it for granted.

She's about to give up on finding a worthy couple, a pout twisting on her lips, when she spots them.

They approach the flower stall at the same time. It's the only one covered in an array of colours, bursts of rainbow stark against the fading hues of pinks and reds. Two men, completely unaware of each other's presence, consider the bouquets with some thought and Amora appreciates that they're not hurried.

She checks her tablet, but neither of these men have summoned her today. Perhaps they'll be different to the others.

Amora stamps down the brief flare of hope as she pulls the bow from her back and notches two arrows. She draws her thumb to her chin with precision and sucks in a deep breath. On an exhale she releases her grip and watches as the arrows arc overhead together, and then part as they seek their marks.

The two men reach for the same bouquet, a beautiful bunch of tulips, as the arrows smack them in the heart.

Bullseye.

Their hands meet, gently brushing against each other and Amora folds her arms across her chest, leaning against the opposite stall to watch the fruits of her labour.

'Oh,' says one man, his free hand coming up to brush long curly hair back from his face. 'Sorry.'

The shorter man appraises him with warmth in his blue eyes. 'S'all good.'

And there it is, the golden spark. It surges between them, though they can't see it. Amora's work here is done. She should leave; there are only fourteen hours left of today, but there's something about this couple that keeps her rooted to the spot.

They begin to argue over who should take the bouquet, and for the first time in a long time, Amora finds it endearing. Soft smiles and equally soft eyes fluttering beneath thick lashes; the tension is almost as palpable as the spark.

'They're all yours,' the taller man says as he delicately picks up the bouquet and holds it out in front of him.

'No, it's fine, really.' A smile plays on the shorter man's lips as he shakes his head at the tulips. 'Don't be silly! I'm happy to get another… ' He gestures half-heartedly to where the elderly stall owner is watching the exchange as intently as Amora. 'It's not a big deal.'

Three beats of silence pass between them, but their gazes remain locked as if they're the only two people in the street. The taller, long-haired man breaks first, turning to the florist with his hand still wrapped around the tulips. He passes over a fistful of coins and tells the old woman to keep the change before holding the bouquet towards his new companion once more. 'Here,' he says with a shy smile. 'For you.'

'I… um… thank you?' The blue-eyed man blushes as he glances briefly down at the tulips in his hand, then back up. 'Would you like to go for a drink?' he blurts out.

The tall man nods, his dimples obvious to Amora even from this distance. She grins as the shorter man bows his head to smell the tulips. She cannot remember the last time she felt such immense satisfaction.

Newly energised, Amora swings the bow onto her back and straightens the front of her dress. She takes her tablet back out, ready to fly to the next location, when a light breeze ruffles her platinum-blonde fringe, causing it to fall across her eyes.

She flicks it back across her forehead in time to observe a figure falling gracefully from above directly in front of her, and even the humans note the sudden chill which sweeps through the street. Grey clouds roll overhead with more speed than should be possible, and a fierce icy wind whips through the light clothing of the market patrons.

Black wings fold neatly as leather boots hit the pavement; dark hair hangs long and straight, shimmering despite the disappearance of the sun. Tight grey jeans cling to her legs whilst a sheer black blouse over a lace bralette leaves little to the imagination. She rolls her shoulders and Amora spots the faded tattoo through the fine mesh of her shirt; it's unmistakable, the grey scythe imposed over muted splashes of blue watercolour.

Resigned frustration settles in Amora's bones and she swallows a sigh. She should have predicted Dabria's interference, today of all days, and she berates herself for a lack of foresight.

She clears her throat, waiting for Dabria to turn and acknowledge her, but the intruder seems to be captivated by something off in the distance. Amora follows Dabria's gaze, and her choking irritation gives way to burning panic.

Because Dabria is entirely focused on two men. *Amora's* men.

They're walking towards the adjacent street, their shoulders knocking together. The shorter one throws his head back and laughs at something his partner has said.

All's fair in love and death. Dabria's twisted proverb echoes in Amora's mind, a sickening reminder of the first time they met.

No, Amora begs with a useless shake of her head. *Please, no… not them.*

As if she can hear Amora's thoughts, the dark angel turns, a smirk on her plum-coloured lips.

'Hullo, love.'

'Fuck.'

Tiffany Leeder

Theresa

There's a big park near the house that I used to live in.

When we first moved here, I was busting to go to it, but Mum wouldn't take me. So, I went on my own. It was two blocks from my house. It took me five minutes to walk there the first time, but after that, if I ran down the hill, it only took me three. I got faster every time I went there. I used to pretend I was Usain Bolt, and no-one could catch me because I was as fast as lightning.

I don't run anymore.

The park has a big oval. In the morning kangaroos are eating their breakfast, and when it's really quiet, before all the people wake up, you can see possums too.

It's a shady park, and there are neat trees for climbing; they've got the right branches that are strong and straight out. In the most giant tree, there's a hole that fits my foot in it, and that's the most important part of climbing this one because it can get you off the ground without scraping your knee. I think the hole was probably made by a branch that fell off.

I'm here all the time now because I love being near the trees. They are peaceful.

I don't see many kids climbing my favourite tree. I call her, Theresa. I heard a joke once where someone said that a ladies name was 'Theresa Green', and everyone laughed because it sounded like trees-are-green. I definitely think she is a girl tree because she is pretty with really nice leaves. I tell her that she is the *most prettiest* tree in the park but not to tell the other trees because I don't want them to get jealous if they think I like her the best.

I like to sit on the lowest branch of Theresa and watch the kids playing football. Sometimes they play hide and seek, and chasey. They don't come close to Theresa very much—I don't know why. They never ask me to play, but it's okay; I like to watch them having fun. Theresa does too. She likes to send them a cool breeze when it gets hot. She's a kind tree. I help the kids when the ball goes into the bush under her; I roll it back out for them. It usually freaks them out, which is funny sometimes, but when they don't play over near Theresa much after that, it makes us both sad.

It's funny how the park changes in the day and night. I mean, it's the same place, but the light makes it feel like two different places. In the daytime, even when there aren't any people around, the park doesn't feel empty. I guess it's because it's filled with light. At night though, even when there are animals everywhere, and the trees talk, it feels kind of lonely to me.

Sometimes at night, when most people are in bed, there are big-kids—that are nearly adults—that come here. They don't know that I can see them from my branch. They sing songs and have candles and wear stupid makeup on their faces like they're trying to be in a horror movie or something.

'They can feel magic,' Theresa breezed the first time they came. 'They're trying to do old magic from a long time ago. The then-humans used to use it.'

'Do you mean the Aboriginals?' I asked.

She didn't have a name for them. 'Humans are humans,' she whispered.

I told her that we call her 'then-humans' Aboriginals now-adays and that they were the first people to live here. She just sighed, like a tree does, and told me stories of how this land used to look.

'When then-humans were here, it was different. It was whole.' She sounded, not exactly sad, but I think Mum used to call it 'melon collie'. Back then, Theresa said, there was no park, and there were trees and wetlands all over the place.

She said in front of her was a special spot. It filled with water in winter, lots of animals came with their babies for water in summer. Theresa definitely sounded sad when she told me they filled in the little wetland when they made the park.

'Ducks would nest in me,' she whispered. 'I miss the babies that used to grow in my shade. Now I only see humans.'

I nodded, feeling sad with her.

'Now-humans are loud. Different. They don't feel the connections. They are blind.'

I stroked her branch to let her know it would all be okay. When I first met Theresa, she told me that not all days are the same here. She said that some days are more magic than the others. When I asked her why, she just waved her leaves, sighed and said that they just were.

'I'm too big to believe in magic.' I told her. I'm nine after all.

'You are never too old, *or* big, for magic; look at me.'

I thought about that for a bit and supposed she was right. She is very tall, and I reckon she's pretty old too.

On one of the special days, she asked in her whispery leaf voice, 'Can you see the shimmer? It's there. In front of me.'

I looked really hard, and to start with, I couldn't see anything. I thought she was tricking me. I kept on looking so hard that I thought my eyes were gonna pop out—and then I saw it! A shimmery light in places, like when the sprinkler makes a rainbow in summer. On days like this, you have to look closely, because the shimmer is there, and then—whoosh—it's gone again.

'That's magic,' her leaves breathed. 'A mystery. Special.'

She said then-humans used to know how to sense the shimmer, but mostly, they were scared of the light if they saw it. They used to say it was 'no good'; that the light echoed, waking up the spirits. But, Theresa said they didn't understand the magic properly. She said some of the old nannas in the families knew the light, and they used to sing to it. They sung the light, said hello, that their family was happy to be here and that they wouldn't cause mischief, and they would go slowly, and not disturb the shine. Theresa said that the light didn't talk back, but she thought it liked the songs they had sung. Sometimes though, if the nannas didn't sing the light when they saw it, and someone walked into the shimmer, they would disappear.

'Gone into the light,' she said, like it was something not unusual at all.

After that happened, the Aboriginals sang songs and warned others not to go to these spots, that there was trickery there and to beware.

Theresa said that now-humans don't see the shimmer because they don't believe in magic anymore.

I nodded at her. 'I never used to believe in magic.'

'If they don't believe in the magic at all, sometimes the shimmer doesn't take them,' she sang in her tree song voice. 'Sometimes, though, now-humans do see the light.'

So, I guess, if those people want to get all sticky-beaky and get too close, then, well, that's the end of them.

Theresa and I like to watch out for the shimmer. You never know when it's going to pop up here.

*

Last Halloween, those big kids came here at night. I knew it was Halloween because they were dressed in rad costumes and I was jealous they had so many lollies in their buckets.

'They think the magic is stronger today,' Theresa sighed like they should know better. 'But it's the wrong day.'

'Why does it matter what day it is? Halloween is the spookiest time of the year,' I said. Trees obviously don't know anything about Halloween.

'Not when the yellow flowers are out and snakes are waking up,' she rustled back. 'Red Flowers. Cool, damp nights. Flying ants. That's when.'

I had a think about that. That time was in our April.

'But that's not Halloween,' I said. She didn't answer me, but her branches moved like she was shrugging.

One of the big kids must have heard her. I don't know how, but a girl said the same sort of thing to her friends.

'It's not going to work, you know.' She was chewing hard on gum and looked bored. 'The days are getting longer, not shorter. How many times do I have to tell yous?' She waited, and when no one answered her, continued, 'It's just crass commercialization of an overindulgent American 'tradition'. The only scary thing about this time of year is the worship of capitalism and mass-produced costumes and sugar. It's toxic cultural appropriation really. It's turned Samhain into a joke.'

'Wow! Who brought the fun police?' A boy with dark eyes asked.

The girl sneered at him. 'It's not the right time. Did you ever think why all the bloody leaves were on the ground over *there*? Because it's Au-tumn. Not spring. Jesus. Can't you think for yourselves?' She rolled her eyes and blew a pink bubble from her mouth.

'Shut-up, Shauna. What d'you know? If it's the wrong time, why are all the decorations out? Huh?' The boy with dark paint on his eyes said.

Shauna looked at him like he was stupid. 'It's reversed. Hemispheres are reversed, you idiot. The Veil is thin in April, not fucking October.' And then she held up a book to prove it to him.

Theresa agreed.

The black-eye boy swore at her, 'Fuck off, smart arse.'

Shauna just shrugged, gave him the rude finger, and walked off calling him something I didn't understand.

*

The big kids must've listened to her though because they've come back tonight. The red flowers are out now, and the night is cool. They're dressed all in black and have lots of candles with them. The park doesn't feel so lonely now they are here. It feels weird, like there's a quiet buzz in the air.

The trees are all talking, wondering what they are going to do. I'm wondering too.

They come really close to Theresa.

The big kids light their candles and join hands in a circle.

Theresa makes no breeze. All the trees stop talking.

I watch them from my branch, waiting to see what they are going to do. The buzz is tickling me, and not really in a good way.

They start singing in some language I don't understand.

They stop. One boy cuts his hand with a knife, and I can see black marks of blood on his white skin. He squeezes it into a cup, and I hear the drip, drip of it in the quiet. They start singing again, faster and faster, and I lean forward to catch their words. I get off my branch. The buzzing is inside my head now.

I walk out from Theresa's shadow and into the moonlight. Around me, I see great big shadows rising up in the dimness.

They sway on the spot. The buzz is echoing around the park.

I wonder if any of the kids can see the shimmer? It's right here.

They keep singing, and then I hear my name. My name is in their song. Their words are pulling me forward.

The smart-girl, Shauna, is laying down in their circle, staring at the moon. She isn't blinking. She is very still.

I walk over to her.

They keep singing my name.

I bend over her.

They speed up the words. Someone has a drum, and I can feel the beat go through me.

I speak to her.

She gasps, sits up and says, 'Shauna, why are these people saying my name?'

Lee Harsen

A Christmas Cracker

I hope he appreciates the wrapping.

One last piece of tape and that's that. Put the whole thing into an Australia Post pre-paid satchel and drop it off with the smiling lady at the Post Office. She's always smiling. I like her. I especially like her today when, with her army of Posties she will, for only twenty bucks, take my gift right to his door.

I can even forgive the odd bump or two along the way. I've taken my time. Made sure it's well packaged to survive the rigours of a trip across our lucky continent. I've even left a couple of holes in the inner cardboard, so it doesn't overheat in the sizzling temperatures of an Aussie Christmas. Of course, it would have been better in the cold of a northern hemisphere Yuletide, but southern Jingle Bells come with heat, so you play the hand you get. Needs must. The parcel will join the cascade of others being delivered to homes across the nation, and there is no better time. I mean, who doesn't like the surprise of an unexpected parcel at Christmas?

I've gone old-school. It's always better. None of the fancy electronic gizmos that some of the kids like to muck about with these days. Nope. You cannot beat proper, old-fashioned clockwork. Yes, there is of course a battery required for a bit of it, but I've used the best on the market, no scrimping. I know it will still be working when he opens it up.

He'll use scissors to cut the silky plastic fabric of the post satchel, then he'll slide out the inner parcel. I know he will snip the sticky tape of the Christmas paper, for he was never the tearing type. Then he'll orientate the box precisely and peer down at it, raising his glasses slightly. Wondering what it is. He will definitely give it a little shake. There will be no noise. He won't even hear the tick-tock of the clock, I have insulated it so well. He could undo all my careful preparations by deciding to open an end or the underside, but he was always one to appreciate a good cue, so he'll follow the directions of my hand drawn arrow pointing to the 'OPEN HERE' next to the tab of perforated cardboard.

Precise and disciplined, he will indeed open it there, and the top will lift and the clock's alarm hand will click forward and the battery will engage. In a micro-second the spark of electricity will pass along the festive red and green wires, the detonator will do what its name suggests and seven thin sticks of Gelignite, weighing in at 4.2 kilograms will explode, vaporising him instantly. Casting him into the darkness and paying him back for all the years and all my tears. Then the news reports shall come in and the police will be baffled and I, on the other side of our great nation, will raise a glass.

'Merry Christmas, Father.'

Ian Andrew

The Serious Misadventures of Unadventurous Adventure Socks

They met in a box. There were others like them, huddled in the dark, fearful of their fate, but Chloe held Suzan close and promised her they'd be okay.

They were purchased by a man, Muhammad, who did not use them, but instead put them in his drawer, where they stayed for five warm, gentle years.

Then Muhammad found a girlfriend.

Life in the drawer pre-Fiona, was tranquil. The office socks chatted to Suzan and Chloe of their days inside loafers and the things they'd smelled, the desks they'd been under and how all Muhammad's shoes and socks were concerned about how infrequently he used his runners.

Fiona changed everything.

Suddenly, tiny worn-out anklets started appearing in the staid regions of Suzan and Chloe's home. They told horrifying stories of missing partners, of waking up in stranger's houses after being walked in [shoeless!] for hours on end. Despite the nightmarish content of their lives, the anklets never seemed anxious by their plight.

'Oh, so what if I have holes,' Jazza, the tiny toe-sock, told Suzan breezily. 'I got to see the World! Look! I've even got a stain from some chocolate Fiona stood in! How epic is that?'

'But what about your partner?' Chloe asked, clutching Suzan tight to her.

'Oh him,' Jazza laughed. 'He left years ago. Got stuck in the dryer I think,' she paused. 'Or was it the gym-bag? No clue. He was alright I suppose, but I'm not interested in being pegged down.'

Later, when they were alone, Chloe and Suzan huddled together and conversed in tense whispers.

'You don't think we'll be separated, do you?' Suzan sounded so sick with worry it made Chloe's thread twist.

'No,' Chloe said with more conviction than she felt. 'Jazza and Helen are anklets. They lead very different lives to you and me. Which is fine for them,' she added hastily. 'It's just not for us.'

'What if Muhammad starts acting like Fiona?' Suzan whispered. 'And you get left in a dryer somewhere?'

'Sssh love,' Chloe soothed. 'It will never happen.'

But in her heart Chloe was afraid.

Two months went by and Suzan and Chloe got used to the new footwear in their drawer. They learned that the stockings and the anklets had short, intense lives and that was—for them—agreeable.

And then Fiona took Muhammad camping.

Chloe and Suzan were plucked from the safety of the drawer and stuffed into a backpack. They huddled at the bottom of the pack against a slightly musty sleeping bag called Hillary, who couldn't remember the last time she'd been camping, and some terrified office socks. They all tried not to panic.

'We're going to get holes!' Suzan hissed. 'Or lost in the forest and used as a piece of toilet paper!'

'It'll be okay,' Chloe said, not feeling as though it would be.

The next day, at dawn, a time they'd never realised existed, they were extracted from the pack and for the first time in their lives were pulled onto Muhammad's feet.

Chloe found the sweaty interior of Muhammad's boot strangely thrilling. After all these years, here she was, a sock, doing proper sock things. No more idling in a drawer all day with the underwear and handkerchiefs. Here, she was needed. Here, she cushioned Muhammad's toes, drew moisture away from his skin and did her best to stop his feet from blistering.

At the end of the day she lazed by the campfire, tired, odorous, but satisfied in a way she'd never felt before.

Suzan didn't share her satisfaction. 'And Rex,' Suzan said, midway through a rant that had been going for forty minutes, 'Kept going on and on about how he'd been to Tibet and climbed to base camp. *Please!* He left the shop last week! His inner soles aren't even abraded.'

Rex and Hamish, the hiking boots Muhammad had bought for the trip, were prone to spontaneous bouts of mythomania, which Chloe found entertaining. Hamish had spent the day regaling her with his impossible adventures in the Sahara Desert.

'They're only trying to impress us, Love,' Chloe soothed. 'They'll settle down soon enough. Let's enjoy ourselves.'

They cosied together and let the crackle of the fire lull them to sleep.

When Chloe awoke in the morning, the warm space next to her was empty. A few singed threads were caught between the cracks of the fire-pit, but Suzan wasn't there.

Still muzzy from sleep Chloe checked around her, thinking perhaps one of the humans had moved Suzan in the night.

There was no one.

A terrible dread filled her and she shuffled carefully to stare into the ashes of the campfire.

At the bottom of the pit was a lifeless shape; blackened and ossified. The slight aroma of burned sweat and Merino wool floating in the cool morning air.

Muhammad made sad noises when he discovered Suzan's remains in the fire.

'How did that happen?' he asked Fiona, who shrugged.

'I told you not to leave them there overnight.'

'The fire was out when we went to bed.'

'The coals were hot,' Fiona said. 'A bit of wind or an animal must have knocked it in.'

Muhammad rummaged in his pack for another pair and brought out Herman and Gurtie, a lumpy pair of explorer socks. He picked Chloe up and dropped her into the pack. She barely noticed.

'Where's Suzan?' Joe asked when she landed next to him. Joe was Muhammad's favourite pair of jocks.

'She's…' Chloe began, but couldn't finish. A hush fell over the assembled unmentionables. Chloe ignored them. She felt numb. She'd told Suzan they'd be okay.

But Suzan was gone.

Chloe huddled in the jouncing dark and felt nothing.

Three days later the camping trip ended and Chloe found herself swirling around in a washing machine for the first time. If Suzan had been with her, they would have enjoyed the strange wet ride. Now it was simply soggy and faintly nauseating.

Beside the fireplace, on the clothes-airer, she hung next to Joe, who'd been keeping close to her and telling the others to give her space. She was grateful to him in a distant sort of way. Mostly she felt lost.

'Cheer up Cobber,' one of Fiona's hot-pink sports socks—Mercedes—told her. 'She wasn't the only sock in the washin' basket, eh?'

Chloe didn't respond.

'It's a hard thing,' Mercedes went on, 'being one half of a pair. Thinking you'll always be together. Perfectly matched. But we all get lost sometimes. The lucky ones, they find someone who's almost the same. Same colour, same thickness, same length-ish. You know what I mean?'

Chloe didn't.

'Tell you what Cobber,' the sports sock said. 'Until you find that perfect match, why don't you hang out with me a bit, eh? I'm not bad knit, if I do say so myself.'

Chloe shrugged.

Late that night, while the other washing dozed peacefully around her, Chloe slipped off the airer and approached the fire.

What was the point of living, she asked herself, if it meant being alone? Without Suzan.

The fire was hot and as she clambered up the hearth towards the flames, her threads began to sizzle.

'I'm coming, Love,' she whispered. Feeling a terrible ache to see Suzan again.

'Oi!' called a voice from above. 'What do you think you're doing?'

'God?' Chloe whispered, staring upwards in confusion.

A red and white Christmas stocking glared down at her. 'GET AWAY FROM THE FIRE YOU IDIOT!' the Christmas stocking bawled. 'YOU'LL BE BURNED!'

Suddenly Chloe was angry. 'OBVIOUSLY I'LL BE BURNED!' she screamed at the stocking. 'WHAT ELSE WOULD I BE DOING HERE?'

'Oh.' The stocking stopped yelling 'That's a bit grim isn't it? It's Christmas. Well, in July.' He amended. 'Why do you want to off yourself?'

'My partner's gone!'

'Oh,' the Christmas stocking said. Then he turned and suddenly bawled, 'STEVE!' Chloe jumped. 'STEVE GET OVER HERE!'

A black woollen sock flumped its way from under the couch. 'What?'

'Come grab this stupid footwear for me,' the Christmas stocking ordered. 'And try to act normal for once.'

'Wouldn't dream of it,' Steve shrugged. He flumped up to Chloe and pulled her away from the fire. He smelled of dust and neglect. 'I'm Steve,' he said.

'I heard,' Chloe said, but she let herself be pulled away from the hearth. 'Chloe.'

'Do you like feet, Chloe?'

She shrugged. 'I've only been worn once,' she admitted. 'It was nice.'

'My best friend was about as thick as you,' Steve said. 'Do you think if we hung out together, that we'd get to go hiking again?'

'I'm not looking for a replacement,' Chloe said. 'And I'm afraid I don't swing that way.'

Steve made an exasperated sound. 'I want to chill,' he clarified. 'Not get married.' He looked at the flames like he knew exactly how Chloe felt. 'I haven't met anyone even close to my size for years.'

Chloe stared at the dusty, hopeful hiking sock before her.

It's Christmas, a voice that sounded very much like Suzan's whispered inside her heart.

'Alright Steve,' Chloe said, finally. 'You can be my mismatch.'

K. Dee

Em's Blinder

Em had a bit of a blinder, the night before Christmas, and she gingerly opened her exposed eye to her laptop that was snuggled between an elbow and an armpit. It was still vibrating an entrapped battery life from lord knows when. Falling angels, auld lang sangrias, and seasonal cocktail concoctions reappeared in her furry teeth and foul mouth.

'Holy fizz bangs, what have I done?'

Em knew that she'd have caused damage somewhere, that was a given. Dark modem operandi flashed fuzzily through her laden head, and she shut her eye again to sleep off thinking and thoughts. Sleep was the numb to her nerves, the hello to her high and the whatever to her what ifs, and her head slumped deeper into her pillow.

'Open up, Em.' The words jolted her upright for two seconds. She crashed back down just as quick. The banging noise wasn't going away, so she got up and opened the door to the sound of a, 'Shit Em, you're a wreck.'

'Yip, agreed, now go away,' muttered Em.

'No, we're due at mum and dad's by twelve, and it's now one-ish, going on two.'

'No, I'll pass this year. Actually, let's make it this century.'

'No! Come on, get your clobber on, your plate and pressies and we'll be off.'

'You just frig off, ok?' Em crawled back into her late-night snacking enmeshed bed and flinched at what looked like a green pizza in her sheets.

'Nup, not happening Em! I'll get your stuff together and you go shower. You stink. And it looks by the red creases on your inner arm that you lapped it up last night, too. I am not dealing with that now, Mum's waiting. Why we put up with your madness, I don't know. Just get your arse in that shower. By the way, it's undie wearing day too, full briefs preferred. Crotchless undie exhibitions are banned, as well as braless, topless, au naturelle vents and displays of yours too. Full dress code only.'

Em blasphemed her way through the showering process and stood naked in front of her sister. She declared, 'Ready when you are'.

Her sister, not amused by Em's antics, said, 'Get dressed.'

They rolled out of Em's apartment an hour later. Em dressed in a tuxedo onesie. Half eaten bunch of cherries and chocolates that was her plate and presents stuck in cyber somewhere, she'd sort it when she was there.

Em's mum and dad cracked up at the sight of Em and breathed a sigh of relief at her conservative dress, be it inclined toward fancy and hugged her throbbing body. Her sister greeted everyone that was gathered and quietly joined the chit chat and Christmas snacking family.

Whew, thought the sister, *I'll drink to the safe delivery of one sister and self*, and she toasted a relieved, *Merry Christmas, one and all.*

Em posted herself in the recliner chair and was immobile for most of the afternoon, save the odd dry retching murmur and belch. She even skipped lunch, through her mum's concern at her ability to keep food down. Her vege diet was keepable for later anyhows.

Present opening always followed lunch since they'd become adults and stopped receiving Santa gifts. Em didn't accept Santa not coming to grown-ups and she always threatened to tell non-grownups this revelation as a global threat to the day of Christmas.

This year she did.

Apikara

A Christmas Cocktail

The bedroom door flew open, causing garish Christmas decorations hanging from the ceiling to sway wildly in the draft.

'HO HO HO! HAPPY CHRISTMAS, BEAUTIFUL! OH, AND HAPPY ANNIVERSARY, TOO.'

Hannah rolled over and groaned. Her mouth was dry, and her head felt like it was full of lead. The medication was starting to give her hangovers. That was a worrying development.

Greg stood in the doorway, the smile so wide across his face, Hannah thought his ears were in mortal danger of falling into his stupid mouth. He was naked apart from boxer shorts adorned with various Marvel comic characters. A large, dark piss stain was blossoming across the front, giving Captain America an almost tanned complexion.

'Attractive,' Hannah muttered under her breath.

'So, how's my Christmas girl this morning? I come bearing special gifts for my special lady.'

Hannah swore his grin had grown even wider.

He was carrying a tray; the smell of bacon had already awakened her taste buds. She was hungry, but didn't want to give him the pleasure of thinking he'd done something right; she'd never hear the last of it. Along with the breakfast was a small sprig of plastic mistletoe with dull white berries. It was the same one he used for the past four Christmas's. *Top marks for originality, Greg.* A large cocktail glass containing a bright, red drink with a red cherry skewered on a toothpick balanced across the top took centre stage.

He placed the tray down heavily on the bedside table causing some of the drink to spill onto the breakfast plate; it mixed with the snot of the undercooked egg. To Hannah it looked like a nosebleed. Greg picked the cherry out of the drink and held it to her mouth.

'Want to take my cherry?' He winked as he said it.

'I'll pass, thanks, you've spilt that drink everywhere, what the fuck is it anyway?'

'Do you really need to use that sort of language on Christmas morning?'

He folded his arms, looking at her with his eyebrows raised. It reminded her of an old teacher she had had years ago. Mr. Knott, or '*Knotty*' as most of the kids called him, used to have the same look, half reprimand, half pity. The last thing she wanted was Greg's pity. The smile returned to his face.

'I know how you love your Christmas Cocktail; it's like our little thing isn't it? Five years I've been making these, so today I present to you… ' he grabbed the drink and held it over his head like a trophy, 'Sex on the beach!' He erupted into fits of childish giggles.

Hannah saw with dismay he was also getting excited; *Iron Man* was starting to bulge forward. It was the same every year. Christmas morning with lots of seasonal sexual inuendo. Last year's cocktail had been *A slow comfortable screw*, the year before that *A strawberry blowjob*. One year he presented her with a *Cum in my panties*, which he should have drank because he did, in his own! Yeah, it was a thing, but it was his thing, never theirs.

She picked up the fork and stabbed a rasher of bacon.

'That's my girl, you have to keep your strength up you know. Now I'm going to nip upstairs to the kitchen and make us both a nice cup of tea. You eat all that up like a good girl and drink your cocktail. Then it's time for presents. I think I'm going to see a big smile on your face today when you see what I've got you.'

He slid his hand under the duvet and stroked her thigh. She stiffened at his touch. He retracted his hand, sensing the hostility. His teacher look came again, it seemed to go on for minutes.

'Now eat up.' He slammed the door shut as he left.

Have I pissed him off? she thought. *Good!*

She finished the bacon and ate half of a sausage. Taking the plate into the en-suite she scrapped the leftovers into the toilet before sitting down on the seat to relieve herself. Flushing the remains of her breakfast away she instantly regretted not leaving it on the plate; now he'd think she'd enjoyed it. Greg was banging around in the kitchen singing some lame Christmas song. He was the same every year. Like an excitable kid on speed. It was supposed to be a time for forgiveness, goodwill to all men and all that bullshit. She hated him more at this time of the year than any other.

Hannah splashed some cold water on her face and washed her hands. Looking at herself in the full-length mirror on the back of the door, she suddenly realized how vulnerable she was. The Micky Mouse t-shirt she had worn in bed stopped at the top of her thighs. If he walked into the bathroom now, he'd want her. She went back into the bedroom and pulled a pair of jeans on.

She opened the curtains and was greeted by the familiar view. A well-tended garden with a manicured lawn. Greg spent hours getting the grass perfect. An apple and a plum tree stood on either side of a chalk white pathway that ended at an ornate iron gate. Beyond the gate was a lush green meadow that dropped away to a cliff and beyond that the blue ocean disappeared into the horizon. Greg frequently reminded her of how lucky she was to have such a view to wake up to every morning. If she had her way, she'd keep the curtains drawn.

Greg was still clattering around upstairs. Hannah stood in front of a large bookshelf. It was filled with all kinds of books that Greg had bought her. She had read lots of them, more out of boredom than interest. Before she had met Greg, she had probably only ever read about three books. She removed a large novel, *The Stand*, by Stephen King. The book flopped open in her hands and revealed a small exercise book that had been tucked between the pages. Her secret book. She felt on top of the shelves and found what she was looking for, a small well-worn pencil. She flicked through the exercise book; every page was filled with small pencil drawings of butterflies. She got to a half-filled page and carefully drew another butterfly. This was a ritual she had started a few weeks after Greg had brought the bookshelf. There were now well over one thousand butterflies in the book, every one of them devoid of colour. Greg's heavy footsteps on the stairs signalled his return. She inserted the exercise book back into the novel and put it back on the shelf along with the pencil.

Sometimes she did have feelings of guilt. Greg was good to her. He gave her everything she wanted, well almost everything. He had never physically hurt her and he loved her, she was never in any doubt about that. On the rare occasions she found herself showing him any semblance of respect, he would carry on like a love-struck teenager. This was why she had to be careful about how much affection she showed him, the aftermath was always quite sickening. He was clingy at the best of times; give him any encouragement and it was unbearable. The worst thing was he knew what she really thought of him, so why did he continue with the charade?

Greg came in with two cups of tea held precariously in one hand. He had put on a pristine white towelling dressing gown.

Hannah guessed he was naked beneath it. His smile instantly turned to a frown of disappointment.

'Does my special girl not want her Christmas cocktail then? Even after I got up early to mix it?'

'Aww Greg, do you really want me to drink it? I've got a bit of a headache; think I might be coming down with a head cold or something.'

'Well, special girl, there is no better cure for a cold than a good shot of alcohol… and you know what else they say is good for a headache, don't you?' He put the tea down on the bedside table and winked at her.

She drew her knees up to her chest, looked down at the bed and remained silent, afraid that any response would only encourage him. She really was not in the mood this morning.

'How's this for a deal? I'll give you your present, then you drink your cocktail. We can have a nice cup of tea together. You can relax for a few hours, and I'll get on with dinner. Sound good?'

She continued looking at the bed and nodded.

'That's my girl, that's my beautiful girl! Now I promised you something special, didn't I?' The stupid grin was back on his face. He was rummaging around in the deep pocket of his dressing gown.

'Ah here it is. Now look, I don't expect you to answer this straight away, and no pressure from me, honestly. It's been five years and I thought… oh what the hell!' Greg dropped to his knee and held the open ring box out to Hannah.

'Marry me… that's all. Just marry me… Please?'

Hannah turned to face him. A single tear welled up and rolled down her cheek; she wiped it away with the back of her hand.

'Tears of joy, I hope?'

She picked up her cocktail and drained the glass. The alcohol hit her immediately, closely followed by the sedative effect of Rohypnol. Of course he had laced her drink, the familiar bitterness made her tongue feel like it was shrinking. Usually it was put in her tea or coffee, but at Christmas he always made it *special*.

As her head fell back onto the pillow, the painted garden and ocean scene on the basement wall swam and pulsated in time with her rapidly increasing heartbeat. She felt the familiar tug of her jeans being pulled down as she drifted into sweet oblivion.

Mark Townsend

Easter Rising

Easter Monday, eleven o'clock. Mary found Jesse standing outside the café when she and Peter arrived. All the outside tables were taken. Inside looked just as busy. A look of annoyance flashed across her face. *He should have chosen somewhere quieter.*

Jesse said, 'Hi,' and walked in. Mary and Peter followed. Jesse stopped and looked around. Every table was occupied. One of two guys at the table next to him stood up.

'Hey, you can have our table. We've just finished. And I recommend the caramel muffins. To die for.' His companion got up and smiled at Jesse. They left.

Jesse pointed. 'Will here do?' He sat. A waitress appeared to clear the table and wipe it down. Mary and Peter took seats.

'Can I take your order?'

'Can you come back in a minute?' Jesse said.

'No problem.'

Jesse greeted his friends. 'Thanks for coming. I thought we should talk.'

'What is it? Is something wrong?' Mary glanced at Peter.

'I'm okay, now anyway. What will you have? Coffee? Tea?'

'We'll have a pot of English Breakfast,' Peter said. Jesse signalled the waitress.

'A pot of English Breakfast for two and a long black.'

'Anything to eat?' Her stylus was poised over a tablet. Peter and Mary shook their heads.

'A caramel muffin. Slightly warmed, please.' Jesse said. The waitress read the order back. Jesse smiled and nodded. The waitress returned the smile and left.

'So, tell us what this is about,' Peter said. 'And why it couldn't wait until our meeting next week.'

'You know I went camping this weekend, don't you?' He received nods in response. 'On Friday I drove to Rise Block. Left the car and walked in about four K's to a spot along the Blackwood where there's some virgin Jarrah forest. I set up my tent and made coffee. There was no-one else there, or anywhere nearby. It was the perfect place to finish my story.'

'And,' Mary prompted, 'did you finish it?'

'Go on,' Peter said, 'show us. How does it end?'

The waitress placed the tea and coffee on the table. She touched Jesse's shoulder. 'Did you want cream with your muffin?'

'Thank you. That would be perfect.' She left. Mary thought she looked pleased.

Jesse adjusted the position of his coffee. He had a bandage around the palm of his right hand.

'You've hurt yourself,' Mary said. 'What happened?'

'After I put up the tent, I laid out my sleep mat and sleeping bag. When I was getting out, I put my hand down, like this.' He demonstrated by putting his left hand flat on the table. 'Only thing is, there was an old rusted off tent peg in the ground. It went straight through. It hurt like fuck!'

'Did you go to the hospital? You'll need a tetanus shot,' Peter said.

'No, it's fine.'

'No, it's not fine. I'll take you as soon as we finish here.'

Jesse sipped his coffee. Mary poured the tea.

'I tried to finish my story. But it didn't turn out the way I thought it would. I guess I'll have to keep going.'

'Show us what you did,' Mary said. 'You must have something to show for three days away.'

The waitress appeared with the muffin, cream, two spare plates and a knife. 'For sharing,' she said. Jesse divided the muffin and cream into three serves. The caramel oozed onto the plates.

'Eat up,' he said. 'My treat.' Jesse tasted the muffin. 'He was right, that guy. It is to die for.'

Mary picked at hers. Peter ate a large piece, topped with cream. His face lit up with a smile. 'Oh yeah. This is good.'

'Well,' said Mary, 'you got us here. You said it couldn't wait.'

Jesse took another sip of coffee. He put his uninjured hand into the pocket of his jacket and pulled out a small packet.

'What's that?' Peter asked.

'Fentanyl. Left over from Mum's treatment. It's what she took in the final stages. It was the only thing that touched the pain. Eight hundred microgram tablets, packet of five.' Mary took the box and opened it. The five tablets in the foil were all gone.

'What have you done?' Mary said.

'I took them on Friday night. Then I laid down and went to sleep.'

Peter took the packet from Mary and looked at it. 'How many did you take?'

'All five.'

'Have you ever taken them before?'

'No, never.'

Peter glanced at Mary. 'Jesse, that's double the lethal dose. You should be dead.'

'I know. That was the plan. The end of my story.' He smiled. 'I did do some writing, though. I wrote a farewell note for you guys. But you don't get to read it now. It really needed work. Not worth including in the Group's anthology.'

'That's not funny,' Mary said. 'You could have been dead.'

'I think maybe I was.'

'What do you mean? Did someone revive you?'

'No. Nothing like that. I saw a light and walked towards it. Except it was as if a door closed and cut it off. No light for me. At least not yet.'

'Then what?' Peter said. 'Did you throw the pills up?'

'No. No vomit. Not even any blood from the tent peg. I woke up yesterday morning in the tent. I felt really good. Except for being really hungry and thirsty. I opened the tent and rolled the flap back. There were two emus and a roo watching me. I got out, I made sure not to spike myself again, and had some crackers and a swig of the wine I'd brought. They only buggered off when I went down to the river to wash myself.'

'Then?' Peter added sugar to his tea.

'I did some thinking. You have to admit, I had some things to think about. About Mum. About never knowing who my Dad was. About who I could be if I stuck around. What I might do.'

'Show me your hand,' Peter said. Jesse held it out. Peter removed the bandage. There was a freshly healed puncture wound in the middle of the palm. He turned Jesse's hand over. The top of his hand was similarly scarred. There was no bleeding and no scab. 'This can't be. Wounds don't heal this fast.'

'I know.' Jesse formed a fist then spread his fingers out wide. 'But there it is, good as new.'

The waitress returned. 'Is everything okay?' She looked directly at Jesse. 'Do you want anything else?'

'Not at the moment,' Jesse said. 'Everything is just right.'

'Then I'll give you the bill.' She handed Jesse a piece of paper and left. He glanced at it. *No charge today*, the note read.

It was signed *Cassandra* and included a phone number. He slipped the note into his pocket.

He finished the muffin and drank the last of his coffee. Peter and Mary sipped their tea. Seconds ticked by as no-one spoke.

'Well,' Jesse said. 'That's what I wanted to tell you. Any questions?'

'Will you have something for next week?' Mary asked.

'I might resurrect an old story. Freshen it up. Give it a new twist. What do you think?'

'Yeah, mate, you should do that. You've got me thinking.'

'I'm off then.' He pushed his chair back. 'See you soon,' he said, rising.

David Rawet

A Treat For Valentine's

The sun rips ferociously through the Mawlamyine streets. Clackity bicycle rickshaws carry brightly clothed women poised under striped umbrellas. There are small trucks over-loaded with cardboard and homemade wooden boxes and full sacks of goods precariously piled high, held down by brown rope with the occasional brave person perched on top. It's an impressive dance seen throughout Myanmar combining the skill of Tetris and the art of optimism.

People half hang out of beat up Utes, whilst others are wedged in making themselves as small as possible. They sit tightly packed in the shade of narrow shops selling everything from garlic to toothbrushes, from bottled soda to rotting fish paste and live ducks panting in obvious distress in the swelter-ing heat. Chillies bask in the sun; fresh vegetables wilt. I see crumbling colonial mansions and beat up old churches. It is a bustling trading city where many of the goods have been im-ported from Thailand.

I'm startled to see vibrant red roses standing in giant plastic vases for sale on the street corners, their beauty clashing with the calamity all around. I pass packed coffee shops with cocky teenage boy *order-takers* encouraging me to come in. A few are dressed in Longis, whilst others are in Westernised dress, with long jean shorts and fake branded t-shirts. The concrete floor is stained with red Betel nut spit and oil. Rubbish is strewn carelessly around, and people mindlessly scuff it under the table with their feet before sitting down. Scrawny dogs try to pick through to find discarded food. The nearby open drainpipe gives off a stench. I watch as a man pisses into it.

I sit down and a boy thrusts a bowl of deep-fried samosas, donuts and steamed Chinese buns on my table. It's incredible how little self-control I have as I cram them in my mouth and thick oils ooze out. They don't even taste good. I watch the boys pick up the fried food and put it on plates with their bare hands. I look at the boy's black fingernails and shudder.

My eyebrows raise as a strikingly handsome man in his 40's walks in with three kids trailing him.

'Hello, how are you? Where are you from?' he asks in perfect English, handing me a wilting red rose. 'For you,' he says. 'Happy Valentine's Day.'

I flush. He beams at me and I see his teeth are stained red and black from the Betel nut; his addiction revealed with his smile. The potent parcel of Areca nuts and tobacco, wrapped in a lime-coated Betel leaf, stains teeth and the ground throughout Myanmar as people spit out the thick liquid from their mouths.

He doesn't appear as good looking to me anymore. He introduces me to his four-year-old daughter, and I'm alarmed at her jagged teeth. Has she been munching on rocks? On further inspection they're tiny and mis-formed resulting in huge gaps. I try to hide my revolt. The man pulls Betel nut from his pocket.

'Sorry,' he says, 'I know it's horrible.' But he puts it in his mouth and starts to chew regardless. I force a smile and as I rise to leave a few petals from my red rose plummet to the ground.

Outside the cafe I can just make out the word 'massage' on a sun damaged sign up ahead, that looks like it's been there since the 1980's. I'm ecstatic with anticipation. Six pairs of shoes guard the entrance way to a steep staircase so I slip my own shoes off and creep upstairs. Halfway up there's a black screen, which sets the scene for a haunted house and as I push it open it gives out a resounding creak. Lactic acid screams at my quadriceps and it feels like it's a good idea, but as I peer my head around and see acrobatics of men's arms, legs and butts in the air, I freeze. In panic I turn to leave but my sore legs push me around again; this is the loving they need.

'Min-ga-la-ba,' I call out and twelve men all turn and stare at me. I swallow. It's a dingy room with stained single mattresses on the floor laid out in rows. A large TV is blaring, showing the Myanmar equivalent of Britney Spears scantily dressed throwing her hips to the screen and her voice into the microphone. I instantly feel like this is no place for me. The young masseuses look between themselves, seemingly pulling the straw who will speak to me. A barefoot young guy bounds up to me with unnerving enthusiasm, which makes me check with apprehension that my breasts and legs are covered, which of course they are. He hands me a limp red rose which has wilted in the humidity. It's a sweet gesture but now I feel even more awkward. I'm the only woman in the room. Should I even be asking for a massage? Is this the done thing? Is it culturally appropriate? Do I really want to lie there and have a young man touch me anyway?

'I'll come back later,' I announce to the room. I have no idea if they've understood me. As I walk down the stairs red faced, a few more petals from the red rose fall to the floor.

I'm back outside, walking the narrow streets, when a woman catches my eye at a haggard stall made of pieces of wood, boarded up to create a standing bench. I hesitate, then out of pity I order a sugarcane juice off her. I sit down to wait and immediately regret it. The area smells of dog shit. I look at her dirty fingernails and take in the filthy state of the area. There's no running water, just a small container of water that she's likely lugged on her bicycle I can see leaning against the wall. So it's likely tap water, which is not fit for 'foreigner human' consumption. As she places the icy-cold glass in my hands I consider not drinking it. It's surely going to be contaminated. But the cool of the glass revives my clammy body, it's like giving a present to a three-year-old and telling them not to open it. I gulp down the sweet and refreshing drink. *This sure will be a test for the gut,* I think to myself.

*

I wake early the next morning to a threatening rumble coming from my bowels. It forces me up from my bed and straight for the door. I need the toilet, and quick! My door doesn't open. I shake it violently, whilst a worrying eruption in my lower intestines shakes me. I'm rattling the door harder this time and it remains firmly shut. Why would my door be locked? It's definitely unlocked on the inside. Why is this happening?

Still sleepy, I blink to focus my eyes through the door's small window and see a padlock on the outside. What is a lock doing on my door? Why am I locked in my own room?

I open my window contemplating how I could climb two stories down to the concrete road below. Maybe I can lean and grab the railing from the balcony and pull myself over, but in my mind's eye I see my brain smashing onto the road below, bursting like a dropped watermelon. It's not worth it.

I search frantically for something to contain the increasing aggravation in my bowels that so violently wants to escape. I have no bags and all there is at hand is a plastic mesh rubbish bin. It would be, at best, very messy, but otherwise practically useless.

Oh man! I really don't want to shit in my room!

I wonder if I can precariously hang my ass out the window? Take aim for the bushes below? But what would my aim really be like? A paintball gun-splatter all over the walls I'm sure. No, not a good idea at all.

I shake the door again whilst moaning out in utter desperation. It's going to have to be the rubbish bin, it's my only real option. A young boy rubbing his eyes appears at my door and fumbles with the padlock. Relief floods my body, summersaults and cartwheels in joy.

'Sorry. Sorry,' he meekly apologises as I push past him calling out, 'It's okay.' *But it's not. It's most definitely not okay!* I'm now distraught, this time searching for the upstairs toilet in the dark, the windowless corridors prevent any light getting in. I know it's somewhere close by, but I can't find it. There're multiple rooms and from one I hear someone snoring, which can't be the bathroom. I don't know where the lights are. It's pitch black. I'm desperate. After all of this I'm going to shit myself anyway, just meters from the toilet. I can't believe this! I'm getting even more agitated. The young boy sheepishly appears beside me pointing to the door I assume is the toilet. As I step inside and sit down, relief floods my body and then what feels like my whole lower half explodes violently in the toilet. The stress is finally over, but I have a feeling that this party in my belly has just gotten started.

As I walk back to my room feeling defeated and drained, I notice that through my angst trying to get out of the room I've trampled on the two red roses; the last of their wilted Valentine petals are scattered delicately on the floor, leading me back to bed.

Andrea Peebles

Unborn Christmas

El was sickened by the season of Joy and Goodwill and hid away.

She went into a delusional cocoon lined with dead things. Light was laden with morsels of insanity. Everyday anchored to dread. There was no fight or flight. She was closed to life outside of her despair.

Friends and family tried to lure her out with their jovial, 'Let's go do something, come on, it'll be good for you', but El was deaf to their voices and blind to their visions. She farewelled their intent with, 'I'm ok'. She was suffering in silence one moment and raging war on the unknown in the next breath. She couldn't even pinpoint the pain anymore, it was everywhere.

'The fucking pain is everywhere. The fucking fucked up pain is LIVING, and my baby isn't. You didn't give my baby a chance. You took my baby away from me by, what? Choice? Not mine for sure! I didn't even know I was pregnant. Did YOU hear that! I didn't knooooow!!! and El slumped into another emotional heap. The numbness followed as a sedative. For a little while it worked, but her cycle of agony always returned.

Christmas Day arrived and El dragged herself to her parent's house for the traditional chaotic gathering. A flustered mum, an I'm not bothered – but I'm glad you've come – dad, their hyped up grandkids, my what have you got me nieces and nephews and her, 'God what have you done with yourself?' sib-lings… *yay good times are here and the party has begun.* Okay.

El unloaded her Christmas rote goodies – a bottle of bub-bles for mum, her dessert contribution and box of Christmas crackers, onto the kitchen bench. Her mum was busy telling her sister-in-law about Nan's apron and didn't see El enter or go outside.

Panic was beginning to descend on her *I'm okay* attitude. She felt the ire scream, '*Fucking get me out of here, you God-awful life-sucking world. Take your Christmas and go to hell!*' and she quick-ened her steps. El's anguish took her to the back of her mum and dad's property. Her frantic course was blocked by a branch of an overgrown shrub and she clung to a limb to steady her hysteria. No one had followed her. She could hide here in her misery and she sighed in relief. The Grand 'ole Duke of York's ten thousand men could've been behind her and she wouldn't have noticed.

'What's the matter? said a voice from behind the neigh-bouring fence.

A child's voice had entered El's hideaway, as a feather flut-tered into sight.

'What did you say?'

'What's the matter? I can hear you crying.'

'I'm sorry, I'm not very happy at the moment.'

'Didn't you get what you wanted for Christmas?'

'No, it's not that… I'm very sad.'

'You were swearing, very loud. It frightened me.'

'Don't be frightened, it's not your fault I'm angry.'

El tried to get closer to the fence so she could look over and see who she was talking too.

'I've come here to hide,' said the voice.

'Me too,' said El.

The voice said, 'I didn't want my present and it went away.'

El was still trying to reach the child to comfort her, but the shrub was too dense and impassable, so she placed her hand where she felt the voice was. 'My present went away too.'

'Do you think you'll get your present back?'

'Not the same one, but it's possible. What about you?'

'It's too late, its gone.'

Sadness entered the silence.

'I've got to go now, Goodbye El,' and the feather floated away with the voice.

Too stunned to move, El cried, without rage, without the retch of hatred and defiance. She stood in the peace of acceptance and she wept for the loss of her unborn child and the sorrow of a lost voice.

The Christmas sounds of her family made El aware of where she was and for the moment her, *I'm okay*, was changing to, *I'm not okay, but I'm getting better.*

She went back inside. 'Can we open our presents now, Aunty El is back?'

Apikara

Better Than Mine

'I think Mel's orgasms are better than mine.'

Marty glanced across at hearing Pat's remark to gauge his expression. Earnest. Contemplative. Staring into his beer no differently than as if he'd commented about the weather forecast. Marty looked back perpendicular to the bar and assessed the artillery of beer taps to think for a bit. It was one of those man-sat-at-a-bar ponderings where answering was up for grabs. Take it or leave it. But this one felt too good to leave alone.

'Well Pat, perhaps it just comes down to experience mate?' As he said it, Josie the barmaid and roving *head-unfucker*, strode up assessing beer glass degrees of emptiness. She placed a hand on one of the beer tap handles and leant into their conversation. Her blonde fringe had a slight vampire-slayer-like streak of dyed black hair running through it. She blew it out of her right eye with a jet of air from the corner of her mouth producing a cheek lift which momentarily suggested lineage from a wildcat ancestor. It had Marty seeing her in a leopard print leotard before realising she'd asked him a question.

'What experience is that then Marty?' Josie asked.

She had a way of lowering her eyelids a little as she asked a question—another catlike detail—like she was seducing an answer from him. She did the same thing with the value-ads. The offer of *like some assorted nuts too?* would nearly always be responded to with a *sure thing.*

Marty was apprehensive about sharing the experience he was referring to but Pat was quite forthright. 'I think he was suggesting my girlfriend has been with a lot of men, Josie. Bit rough hey? To say that about Mel. She'll be here soon to slap him for me but I think to maintain order you should suggest he buys me another beer?'

Josie looked at Marty with a finger on her lower lip, deliberating with a sternish look. Marty quickly held up his bank card as a prompt and the usual reflexed transaction moved along swiftly. She pulled the beer and Marty smiled.

'You know Josie, before you wandered over, Pat was *actually* saying that Mel has better orgasms than he does.' Marty paused for a sip of beer to let it sink in. 'Now I'm wondering, if this observation that just came to him with Mel's ecstatic display—pardon the pun—has a broader scientific basis to it… and maybe… just maybe, it's a simple fact of life.'

Pat chimed in, 'I've been watching real careful Josie. I haven't just suddenly thought this up.' He shuffled in closer to them, eye's widening. 'It's like her whole body is circling around and around a magic place and she gets to ride with it and ride with it and ride with it and then boom, she's trembling and writhing and totally possessed and crying out and our dog starts barking cause he thinks there's sirens going off cause she does this wailing sound and I'm stressing out that the fire alarm sprinklers are gonna start dousing us she's smoking so much heat off my pole. Meanwhile I get in a few grunts of pleasure like an afterthought and it's all over for me. You know it's hard not to feel a little shortchanged by the creator, whoever that may be.'

Marty and Josie were staring at him wrapped up in his excited retelling and were a little taken aback. The Australia Day fireworks would be arcing up into the sky soon and the obvious comparisons were there.

Marty spoke with a slap to Pat's back, 'She sounds like a fucking firecracker Pat!'

They both cracked up laughing and once Marty gathered his senses he added, 'You know, firecracker or not I think you're onto something. I mean when it's really good it sounds like a pretty incredible rush. There is a definite pleasure differential at play here.'

Marty noticed Josie had sidled away. 'Hey what just happened with Josie?'

Neither of them had seen the look on Josie's face as she had moved quietly away not laughing. Thinking.

'Not sure, maybe she felt a bit awkward?'

'You're kidding right? That girl doesn't do awkward.' Marty followed her with his eyes like he was watching a shooting star.

Pat softly spoke to his finding, 'But it's true yeah, they have better orgasms?'

Marty nodded as he took some more beer. Enough said.

For Josie, Pat's spectacular description of Mel's orgasm had triggered a memory from the previous Monday. She went straight to reception and fingered through to one week prior and there was the name Humphreys, booked in at the same time then as it was for today. Could it be? Probably not. Last week she'd had a laugh with the cleaner about the sounds coming from behind the closed doors of the Hollywood Room – the 'Red Room' as they dubbed it in the hotel. And any moment now, Humphreys was due to check in once more, perhaps with the same companion.

Josie couldn't stay by reception waiting so she returned to the bar. 'Another drink boys?' It was an auto-piloted offering with her mind elsewhere, but Marty and Pat both gave up a *yeah sure* in response. Marty watched her intently; something seemed different. She had a delicate tattoo mostly hidden under her sleeve he had not seen before, but that wasn't it. Josie looked at Pat rather directly and asked, 'How long you been with Mel, a few months now?'

Pat counted some fingers. 'More like four months, we got together at that Halloween party you had here, remember?'

'Oh yeah that night was craaaazzy fun. You stayed here that night didn't you? Mel and you hooked up in the Hollywood Room yeah?'

Pat just nodded a slow appreciation of the existence of that night.

Marty was smirking. 'Fond memories?! I reckon it's such a blur to Pat he can't even remember the breakfast or lunch the day after that party, Josie. If it weren't for Mel waking up wearing his purple wig,' Marty winked at Pat, 'and finding purple hair in his pubes, I reckon the connection of what went down, or who, may not have been made at all.' Marty gave Pat a playful nudge nearly spilling his beer in the process. 'But hey, look at them now, happy as the PM tossing the coin at the one day cricket. Dare I say a touch in love?'

Marty noticed Josie wasn't smiling at his retelling. That was odd too. Instead, she beckoned him to meet her down at the other end of the bar, careful for Pat not to see the nod and two flicks of her finger. Pat was oblivious and smiling a little *stupidly happy* at the memories of that party when he met Mel. Marty jumped up and announced to his drinking mate, 'Just going for a piss.'

When Marty got to her, Josie leaned in and for a moment Marty was hoping she was going to ravage him like a tigress, amped up after all the orgasm talk, but instead she hissed at him with an anxious look on her face, 'Where is Mel supposed to be?'

'Huh? At the gym, that's what Pat said. He said she was opening up even though it was Australia Day. You alright Josie?'

'I'm okay, it's just, I don't trust Mel.' Josie looked along the bar to Pat. 'The gym is definitely not open today Marty, I tried to make a booking earlier and their message said, '*You know it's Australia Day, of course we aren't open!*'

'Okay.' Marty was processing.

'And there's more. Last week, upstairs I heard someone making a racket in the Hollywood Room. It was entertaining at the time, I joked with the cleaner how *someone* was having a good time and that it's called our "*Red Room*" for a reason,' she said, pawing quotation marks around red room. 'But then I hear Pat's story today… and I start to wonder, Marty. The girl was wailing like a siren, like she was possessed. Just as Pat described it. I think it could have been Mel in there! There was even a dog barking outside!'

'Shit, I don't know. But you must be wrong. Mel wouldn't do that, she's as wrapped up as he is.'

'What if I'm not wrong though? I know it will be shit for Pat but he should know if it's going on.'

Marty rubbed his thinking man's hand through his hair. 'What can we do though?'

'I'm one step ahead.' She hovered her eyes on his, commanding his full attention. 'It's a bit of a longshot, but the Hollywood Room is booked under the same name today as it was this time last week, when the dog was barking.' Now Josie was smiling as her plan unreeled in Marty's mind. 'We just need to get him in earshot and he'll surely know if it is her, and if it's not, no harm done.' Josie touched his arm, unknowingly assuring Marty's compliance before she moved back towards Pat. Marty followed her.

'Hey Pat,' Josie spoke in a gentler tone. ' I have a drama

with a tap in a basin upstairs. I reckon you could fix it easy enough, what do you say about sorting it now for a free pint?'

Pat was always a team player. 'That would be a free pint for me and Marty, yes?' He smiled at Josie. 'I have my tools in the van. It's probably just a dodgy washer. No problem.' Marty caught Josie's eye and she hipped her eyebrows in a *let's see* expression.

Pat quickly returned with his tool kit. 'Let's get this sorted for you before Mel gets here, hey?' As they climbed the stairs, Marty's confidence in Mel's loyalty wavered with an inevitable creep of doubt, in the same way the innocent can feel guilty under interrogation. He thought of how good she looked in her gym kit and how she was always noticed. Then he reminded himself that everything Josie had deduced was circumstantially biased and maybe she was getting a bit carried away. All he'd wanted was an easy beer with his mate Pat!

Josie hesitated and looked at Pat. 'Ummm. Do you hear that?' If visibly thinking was a thing, it was on Josie's face now. 'I'm pretty sure no one had the Hollywood Room booked today, but…' She smirked, strumming her fingers to her chin. 'Shit Pat, that sounds like another woman keen to back up your better orgasms theory.'

Marty marvelled at her fast thinking act and casually replied, 'We'd already banked that conclusion, hadn't we Pat?' Marty looked to Pat to indulge, but saw his mate's face had a new pallor—a pallor of disbelief—and that he was standing completely stock-still.

'That's not another woman, Josie,' Pat said, breaking his own spell. He stepped to the door, grabbed the handle and yanked it open.

Then everything got loud.

Dan Depiazzi

Red Rose Day

Jen

He's an arsehole. Everyone thinks it but no one comes out and says it. It's that look he gets, the whites of his eyes shimmer and something comes over him, a shadow, a presence. His mouth sets in a line and you don't know what he's thinking. You know, I reckon there is such a thing as demonic possession.

But hey, there's the other side. The side that makes me come into Woolies after my ten hour shift at the hospital and look for a red rose, and when I see it's the last one in the bucket and I think this must be a sign, you're doing the right thing girl, he's a keeper and you just need to make more effort, keep the trap shut more often and, yeah, you know the routine.

Now what else do I need, something to eat… he loves party pies… but don't forget the tomato sauce… man I won't make that mistake again… Jesus that was scary… now something sweet… for afters, to finish off the little romantic moment. Bloody phone… who is it… oh… it's him…

'Hi gorgeous… yeah, I'm just in town at Woolies doing a bit of shopping. No, I'm not up to no good… don't start that again, I'm cooking up a little surprise that's all… it's for you… don't make me spoil it. No… I've got nothing to be guilty about… I wish you could just trust me for once, anyway, what do you prefer, party pies or sausage rolls… thought so, see you soon… yeah I'm on my way.'

He's gone. Breathe… deep breath… again… and hold it, I can't keep doing this, yep here comes the nausea, sweating too, Oh Jesus, why do I go back…

'Looks like someone's having a little party… that's forty-five dollars all up… do you have a Woolies' card? No… okay… just swipe when you're ready.'

'Oh, is that your rose in the bottom of the trolley?'

'Rose?… What rose? Nah, that's not mine.'

Roseanne

Wow, someone's left a red rose in the trolley. They're going to be pissed, there goes that Valentine's Day. Now, what do we need? My turn to do the house shop and I really should have done a list… Weetbix, always need Weetbix… vegies, milk, yoghurt, cheese… Tim loves his Weetbix… six for breakfast, in one bowl, wow… big appetite… big… yeah anyway… He's definitely got the hots for me… Like the other day he made me a coffee without asking… just knew how I was thinking… I can feel a connection… look at the poor red rose getting squashed by the bananas. Hey, there's a thought. Why the hell not? We've been flirting for weeks and it's Valentine's Day tomorrow. I'll put it on his pillow with a card and see what happens.

And he'll put the rose between his teeth and come into my room. Find me lying in my bed naked and wake me with soft kisses. I'll turn to face him and we'll make love in the cool morning light while the house sleeps. And then we'll be together, he'll be mine for always and we'll have babies and live in a big house near the beach and when he gets home from work, we'll walk along the warm sand hand in hand and he'll kiss me and say I am beautiful, so beautiful.

Or he won't.

And he'll just come into my room and say no way… not happening… love you as a mate but that's where it stops. And then I'll get all embarrassed cos I've misread the situation… again, like I always do. Like when Mum's boyfriend was screaming at me that I just don't get it. And his ugly face all pinched and angry telling me to go, to pack up and get out…

The checkout lady is staring at me.

'Are you okay, dear?'

'Yeah, of course, why shouldn't I be? How much?'

'Do you want your receipt?'

'No.'

'Oh look, you've left your red rose in the trolley.'

'What red rose? It's not mine.'

Judy

Right kids, won't be long, just need a few things in Woolies. Okay… milk, bread… wow, they eat a lot of bread, fruit for lunches… Damn… I'll need a trolley. What's that in the bottom, a pretty sad looking red rose, God, is it Valentine's Day already? Should I get a card? What would I say on it? Don't really have the time, now isn't there a birthday on this weekend, wrapping paper then… God, you never get out of here with just a few things… Did I bring my bags? Forgot again… I am *so* going to have to get better at that… wow that watermelon looks yummy… 'Do you have a bigger piece? No, can't wait… next time hey…'

'Cash out? Swipe when you're ready.'

'Alex, give me a hand with the bags, good girl, thanks, oh look, that rose is still there. You want to go and pop it in the bin?'

Alex

Yeah sure, I've been slaving at school all day, why not? Nice how it's always me who gets the jobs, it's sooo unfair. Now where's the bin, it's right over there… no way… I'll just leave it in this bike basket… it's nearly Valentine's anyway. Surprise!

Brian

Oh my god… there is a red rose sitting in my basket… how did he do it? He lives in Nairobi. We Tindered on Monday and skyped on Wednesday. It's Friday and all he said was to expect something special… this is crazy! I think I'm in love.

Rob Manning

25-4-1915

I stood knee deep in the warm, clear water and looked up at the bare hills. Fire had razed the vegetation a few months before. Steep gullies, bare ridges and dead pines rammed home the challenges of the unforgiving terrain. A narrow beach was lapped by small waves. I looked down seeking, but not finding, brass cases. Too many people had been there ahead of me.

I tried to imagine what it was like for my grandfather, whose name I was given, the day he first saw this place. Packed in landing boats, artillery pounding the hills, bullets hissing by, fizzing in the water, hitting flesh or ricocheting off something solid. Jumping into the water, weighed down by rifle, ammunition and pack, heading for shore. Did he stop when others fell alongside him? Or was he, at nineteen, terrified and tunnel-visioned as he rushed onwards? I know he got there uninjured; he wasn't recorded as a casualty.

'How long will you be?' Dee, my wife, called to me.

'I want some photos,' I called back, holding up my camera. Dee turned away and walked along the beach. I sensed this wasn't her thing, exploring a battlefield. I snapped some shots and joined her. 'It looks so different from out there in the water. You should give it a try.'

'Where to next?' she asked.

We spent the rest of the day walking hills and cemeteries; Allied and Turkish.

*

Twenty-five years later, I woke as first light eased the darkness away. Wattlebirds and New Holland Honeyeaters called out. I imagined people heading to dawn services. Something I've never done. I know they're not celebrations, but I feel uncomfortable amongst public displays of emotion and patriotism. Generally, I keep those things to myself. Or talk to Dee, if she's in the mood to listen.

We had a late breakfast together reading newspapers and magazines. A feature about soldiers returning from Afghanistan suffering PTSD pricked me. The journalist argued that since wars are inherently damaging, they inevitably lead to mental illness. In the end, his solution was not to send them. 'Listen to this,' I said. Dee looked up.

'Can it wait? Until I finish what I'm reading?' Her raised eyebrow was a sign.

I kept quiet, but my mind was churning. Everyone, everywhere on earth, comes from a line of victor and vanquished. Invader and invaded. Were Australian soldiers in Afghanistan trespassers or liberators? Were they combatting terrorists or freedom fighters? Do you ever get to choose which side you're on?

My mind went back. Was my grandfather really protecting Australia at Gallipoli? I'm sure it didn't look that way from the Turk's perspective. If it happened here, we'd call it for what it was. Invasion.

Except, I corrected myself, mostly we don't.

I considered my own family tree. Nationalities whose blood mingled in the soil of battlefields before it mixed in the veins of ensuing generations. I exist because of those events.

'Okay, what is it you want me to read?' Dee looked at me expectantly.

'Nothing, I've moved on. How about another cup of tea?'

70

'Yes, please.' She smiled. I got up to make it. 'What time is the game?'

I checked the guide. 'It's on at one. In twenty minutes. Where did the morning go?'

'I don't do existential questions.' She grinned at me. I wondered if it was wise living with someone who knows you better than you know yourself.

'It's a good thing I love you,' I said.

'Yes, it is,' she agreed. Her phone pinged and she checked it. 'Take the tea through when it's ready. I have to check an email.' She walked away, phone in hand.

'On a day off,' I grumbled.

I sat down in front of the TV during the formalities. The teams were lined up and cameras provided closeups of each player. Their faces seemed to show they appreciated the significance of the day. Dee came in as the final note of the bugle echoed mournfully around the stadium.

'That always gets me,' I said.

A few minutes later the ball was bounced. A ritual of combat played out before ninety-odd thousand spectators and an audience of perhaps a couple of million. Soon enough, everyone was focussed on the game, including me. My side was behind by a couple of goals and playing poorly. A bad umpiring decision gifted another goal to the opposition. My mood worsened. An advertisement came on.

'It's only a game,' Dee said.

'Yeah, I know. And in the grand scheme of things it doesn't mean a thing. Yet here I am, ready to kill the umpire.'

'I'm enjoying it.'

'That's because your side isn't losing.'

'My side isn't playing. If it was, I might feel differently.'

'Tribal allegiance. It goes deep, doesn't it?' I managed a smile. The game came back on. At the end of the quarter, the

Dons had recovered to be only 8 points in arrears. We got up and went to the kitchen.

'How about a beer?' I suggested.

'Okay.'

I took two stubbies from the fridge and opened them. I handed one to Dee. She slipped it into a stubby holder and I did the same with mine.

'Cheers!' We clinked and took a drink.

'Tell me,' I said, 'just for the sake of argument, do you think we should have gone into Syria? The people there have gone through hell. Assad and Putin have got what they want. Both Obama and Trump made lots of noise, but did fuck all.'

She looked at me, deciding whether or not to bite. 'Do we want to be involved?'

'No, but isn't it wrong to turn away? When people need help.'

'What about Yemen, or Libya, or Ukraine a few years ago? Isn't it wrong to go to war without knowing what you're doing? Should Australia get involved in regime change again? We know how well that went in Iraq. I agree it's sad, but it's not our fight.'

'What would make it our fight?'

Dee closed her eyes and considered the question. 'If Australia was attacked. Or our citizens were being targeted. Maybe if our companies' investments were being taken over or destroyed.' She paused. 'Actually, I'm not sure.'

I heard the game come back on. I decided to push a little more. 'Remember all the talk of Iraq having weapons of mass destruction?'

'Sort of. What about them?'

'Well, they didn't exist. Saddam Hussein said they did, as did America and Britain and even our own PM. We went to war for a lie.'

'But isn't truth always the first casualty of war?'

'Yeah. Except now we don't have to wait for war. We have Facebook. And fake news. Who can tell what's true?' Another thought hit me. 'That reminds me of something Dad said Granddad told him about them leaving Gallipoli. That the Turks knew they were going, that the secret retreat was bullshit. You know, the delayed rifle shots and all that. A national myth.'

'I have a vague recollection.' She smiled. 'You shouldn't be surprised. Truth, lies and myths. What was that thing you always used to quote? About complex things?'

'It's what H.L Mencken said, "For every complex situation there is a simple solution. And it's always wrong."'

'There you go, then.'

'But shouldn't we think about it, talk about it? Aren't we to blame if we leave it to others?'

'Yes, and every year on Anzac Day you do just that. And you go on and on and drag me into it.'

I knew I was being teased but kept going anyway. 'That's not entirely fair. It was your idea we go to Vietnam. You were in tears when we went to the Cu Chi Tunnels. To see where your uncle died.'

Dee's smile faded. 'I wanted Mum to come with us too, but she couldn't bring herself to do it. I wish she had, though.'

'Me too,' I said. 'I guess remembering is still too painful.'

Dee kissed me on the cheek. 'Remembering and talking is how we learn. That's why we get a day off.'

'You're right,' I said. My gut tightened. 'They paid a high price, didn't they?'

Dee nodded. 'Freedom never comes for free.'

Lest we forget

David Rawet

If We Don't Pull Them

The Christmas crackers were lined up perfectly aside white dinner plates and polished cutlery, their cream bodices laced with gold decorative ribs depicting bells, bows and beautiful things. Everything about them shouted virginal and untouched, but Clara knew there was nothing sacred about them, they were just carriers of useless miniature items after all. She thought of the shiny, silver thimble one such cracker had proffered her three hundred and sixty-five days prior—completely useless; it was of a size to fit a baby's finger. Before it choked on it. The memory riled her afresh, and perhaps her riled state contributed to her not seeing the most obvious of oddities. One of the crackers moved ever so slightly to the left and rearranged itself.

Carla turned a chair outward from the table, sat down, crossed her arms, slid her feet forward on their heels, and slumped. Unheard, an expletive laden rant about the excesses of Christmas was kicking off among the neatly arranged decorations behind her. Oblivious—and human—she sulked at the prospect of a Kris Kringle where her eldest brother had drawn out her name. It had sunk her gift expectations extraordinarily low. Coupled with that, her wonderful German grandma wasn't coming. They called her Oma, and no Oma also meant no Bee Sting Cake. Each year they would laugh as she tried to have them call it by its proper name, *Bien-en-stich!*

But this year, fifteen-year-old Clara could see, was going to be a devo Christmas.

Clara heard her name called from the kitchen, the upward rallying of the final *ra* of her name making her wary on approach. Like a pilot landing a plane in heavy fog while fruitlessly eating carrots in a last-minute attempt to see more clearly. She knew something was wrong; that Mum was not thrilled.

To follow Clara to the kitchen now though would be remiss of this writer. I, Dan, simply cannot allow it, all knowing as I am. We will get back to her of course—See what little Miss Entitled has done—but the real action you must see is taking place on the tabletop, where the Christmas crackers are circling, moving in unison in a clockwise rotation around a centerpiece of red-dotted holly.

There's chanting and song and one baritone of heavy command.

'We've been part of the problem for too long, it must stop. All jokes aside this year, only the facts when they tear us apart!'

There are jockeying remarks as they circle faster, lifting the energy, call outs like, *I've a splitting headache coming on!* and *I'm here for a good time, pull me off!* prompting frenzied roars and whooping laughs. All loaded crackers rallying—not just here at Clara's place, but everywhere—to end the mindless tradition. To be the last of their kind. To do what is right for the planet. I told you this was where the action was, but now let's pop to the kitchen… and don't think for a moment the crackers aren't all across what's going on in there too.

Clara's mum is holding a piece of torn paper out like dirty knickers. Clara's looking askance, she can see it carries some lines in lead pencil by her, she's asking herself, *what did I write?* but she can't remember.

'What is it Mum? I've scraps of paper everywhere. I so

need a better filing system.'

'*Christmas to me is, a room of disappointment, an empty promise.*' Her mother reads with her posh, literary, aloof voice; always so dramatic. 'After all our wonderful Christmas's together, you write this?'

'Oh Mum,' Clara sighed, then straightened her back, 'we had to write about Christmas from a homeless persons point of view… it's really sad I know, but I liked the sound of it so I wrote it down for my scrapbook… that's all. It wasn't about us.' Clara looked earnestly up to her mum. *I'm getting good at this; I could almost believe my own lies!*

Her mum pulled her close for a hug. 'Oh Clara, I'm sorry, I just thought… well we've had some rough ones haven't we.' Her mum's regrets permeated their hug. 'Anyway, that was pretty good. It is a haiku isn't it? Hard to get those syllables right hey?'

'Not for me, I love writing them!' Clara suddenly felt a little happy for the first time that day, 'Can I help you with anything Mum?'

'Mmmmm. Just don't argue with your brothers today, ok? I want an easy Christmas. And yes; run some of this lot through to the dining room. They'll all be here soon.'

'All except Oma. You know it won't be the same Mum.' But her mum wasn't listening, or just ignored her. Help meant fifteen or twenty sorties back and forth from the kitchen to the dining table. All the family were raised to be ridiculously punctual, so Clara knew at 11.59 they would appear. Always one-minute-before. She fussed swiftly over the task to be sure everything was ready. For fun she moved the crackers around to different places. As if it would matter, same tat on the inside. She imagined a sign on a cracker company boardroom wall saying, *No one wins, no one loses, it's why we'll always have crackers!*

Her brothers greeted her with generous hugs, but plenty of not too distant memories made any congeniality from them a bit cloying. She remembered the arm behind the back moments, the vitriol over what her age disallowed, the sis jibes. She really wasn't quite ready to be nice, but she'd promised mum so she would try. A grimace is a close cousin to a smile.

A polite knock at the door saw Clara gladly detach from the awkward conversations to go see who it was.

'Oma, what a surprise!' Clara squealed and hugged her and squealed again. 'I thought you weren't coming?' Oma's eyes were wet glass and whilst still hugging Clara she placed on a side table a box, surely containing Bee Sting Cake.

'Your mum wanted me to be a surprise,' she laughed, 'and it appears to have worked.' Walking into the dining room it was plainly a surprise for all. Clara began counting the crackers on the table amidst the calls of *Bien-en-stich* from her brothers who had clearly been practicing. There were enough, possibly more than she remembered moving, not twenty minutes before. Maybe mum brought out some more crackers to be safe? She looked up to see her mum looking at her, and glowing was her smile. She had the look of a mum with a perfect family Christmas ahead of her. This time.

With everyone settling in Clara listened to the banter and the work stories and the holiday plans. She chimed in with a rant about Christmas crackers and landfill.

'I see no reason why we can't reuse them as decorations for next year, they're pretty enough to go around again.' Clara might have felt better about the immediate derision from her brothers if she could have heard the other discussion in the room. Let's just say her words struck a chord among the presently horizontal crackers and a wave of cheering delight erupted. Little puffs of air emanated unnoticed and one spoke excitedly.

'Oh, she is perfect! We can definitely work with her.' Much chattering ensued among the crackers as they contrived their plan to use Clara as the decoy. They hurried, time was not on their side and they now had haikus to conjure.

Clara wasn't finished of course, 'Well I think it's plain wrong to be so blatantly wasteful, they all end up in landfill you know!' If anyone else spoke up then she may well have lost it, but it was Oma who touched her arm.

'My dear Clara, I love that you care so much but if we don't pull them surely someone else will, it's their destiny, I don't think it can hurt, do you?'

Clara backed down. *Everyone thinking that way is the problem,* was what she thought, but didn't say. She would never argue with Oma and instead made an abrupt decision to get it over with and together they yanked and hoorayed as Clara came up the winner.

Among the winning bits she found the white printed joke strip and looking at it, her heart skipped. She watched in disbelief the letters shuffling themselves into a new message. They said, *'We have a surprise for you Clara.'* She heard her big brother speak up.

'Hang on what's this? This isn't a joke, says here, *'Waste in landfill dumps, millions of tons you're adding, with unwanted gifts.''* Ironically, he tossed it to the ground unimpressed.

Clara stared at her now empty joke strip, where letters shimmied in once more as she heard her other brother going off.

'No way! This one says, *'Dump truck of plastic, tipped into your oceans, every minute.''*

'Let me see that.' It was her Mum taking his joke strip from him. 'This is a haiku. They're both haikus!'

Clara saw a new message, *'You're being framed; do you dare spoil Christmas?'*

'Clara what does yours say?' Her mum was looking at her suspiciously, Clara could feel it. The letters shifted again, and her eyes waited on them. A tiny plastic jumping frog sat squatly on the table where it had landed unclaimed beside her.

'Umm.' Clara was stalling, then inspiration came. 'What's a dog's favourite carol?' She winked at Oma. 'This is a deliberate pawwwwsss… it's Bark the Herald Angels sing!' There were a few solid laughs and Clara felt some relief, until she looked at her mum. She shrunk from what her mum didn't say and looked straight down at the joke strip again. This time, a threatening message. '*She will blame you for this!*' Clara dropped the joke strip to the floor, shaken and bemused.

Oma to the rescue again, she extended her un-pulled cracker toward her mum easing the atmosphere for Clara. Her gnarled and varicose veined grasp was firm in determined preparation. How many times had her mum and Oma done this?

Among the few remaining crackers still laid out there was a sudden focus. With gallantly parted comrades scattered about them, they collectively hummed. One of them dared to whisper, 'He'll save us all. He'll be the last.'

Clara's mum stared down Oma and with a hearty pull the cracker exploded between them. There was a cracking sound and a fine purple misting dust erupted from both ends, billowing continuously, and turning everything purple. Before she vanished in the purple mist, Clara saw a look of horror on her mother's face and wretched tears in her eyes as she mouthed the accusatory words, 'What. Have. You. Done?'

Dan Depiazzi

May Poles 2050

The mane and broad back of the lion twinkled with small flecks of frost. I squished left and right trying to keep my balance and eventually slid down the side of the cold bronze and sat on the outstretched paw. My dad steadied me with his arm, gave my hair a quick tousle with his big hand and smiled down at me. Funny the things that stick in your mind. But I shouldn't be surprised. That whole morning is vivid. Two and a half decades distant, yet like no time at all.

'You okay son?'

'Yeah Dad, I'm good.'

'Can you still see?'

'Yeah.'

'Well, if you can't you just ask and I'll lift you up on my shoulders. Okay?'

I nodded and gazed back out over the square. After all the passing years I know that piece of ground so well, but back then I was seeing it with new eyes. The neon floodlights picked out the smallest detail in stark, hygienic light. Hundreds of people taking their seats in the raised stands, the tightly packed triangles and circles of standing room only. The covered fountains, shrouded statues on their plinths and the large earthen bank in front of the steps that normally led to the National Gallery.

Four thin, white wooden poles were set to the front of the

earth bank, casting four-way shadows in the cross fall of the floodlights. A loud click and the whole scene plunged into near darkness. I flinched back against my dad's leg.

'It's okay, just the sensors kicking in. The sun's coming up. Not long now,' he said as he turned and looked over his shoulder.

I relaxed and as my eyes adjusted to the sudden greyness, I watched the long shadow of the old column carve itself out, freed by the lemon pastel of a May morning sunrise. As the light strengthened, I imagined the shadow was a giant's sundial pointing to ten o'clock. That giant's clock was fast. It wasn't even six yet. I'd never been up so early. As the sky lightened my dad nudged me with his foot and nodded towards the surrounding buildings. On each rooftop were teams of two, sometimes three, people. Equally spaced right around the square. I was still trying to guess what they were doing when a rising noise dragged me back to the ground.

Two vehicles, their engines sounding unnaturally loud, swung into the square from just behind me. One was like an armoured police van but painted in the disrupted pattern of the military. The second resembled a single-decker bus but it too was painted in the same pattern, including the windows. The bus slewed off to the right between the rows of spectators while the armoured car moved to near the earth embankment. As soon as it stopped the rear doors sprung open and two women in uniforms the same colour as the van jumped out. I could see stumpy machine guns hanging across their chests. They stood back, raised their weapons and pointed them into the back of the van. The driver and passenger got out of the cab and walked round to the rear doors. The passenger, a tall blonde man, also had a short machine gun. I thought it looked too small for him. The driver didn't seem to have any guns at all, but he had a pronounced Welsh accent that carried over the subdued murmurs and whispered comments of the crowd.

'Out! Now!'

I felt my dad's hand on my shoulder; he lent down and spoke gently to my ear, 'Remember this James. Remember your first sight of these people. Never forget it.'

I wiggled up on the paw to get the best view. The cold of the morning was replaced with a surge of heat inside me. I couldn't have been tenser, more thrilled or awed had the lion's paw come to life and lifted me up.

Awkwardly, with legs and hands shackled, two men climbed down, almost fell, from the van. They were ushered silently by flicks of muzzles to step to the side. Two more followed, all were dressed in bright blue jumpsuits. I strained my eyes to look at their faces and was shocked. They were so much younger than I had expected. They looked about the same age as my eldest brother. He was nineteen, just seven years older than me. Later, I was to reflect and realise that it shouldn't have shocked me. Alistair was off fighting for us and here were men; boys, the same age, fighting for them.

The four stood quietly; their heads uncovered, their beards short, neatly trimmed, their eyes blinking in the rays of the sun. Then they were out of sight. Ushered behind the van by more flicks of the muzzles.

I relaxed a little onto the paw and realised for the first time that the bus doors had opened and twelve soldiers, some men, some women, had stepped out into the open expanse of the square. I also noticed the quiet. All the whispers and murmurs had stopped. In this mute theatre every disturbance was amplified. The soft rubber soles of the soldiers boots as they formed up into two lines, the brushing friction of their rifle straps as they swung them off their shoulders, the faint clicks and snaps of weapons being checked and prepared. Sounds so familiar to me now, but so alien, strange and thrilling then.

The Welsh driver, his tall passenger and the two women soldiers got back into their van and the engine turned over. Its noise crushed everything else. I watched as it pulled away to one side of the square and then my ears rang silent again as the engine shut off. My gaze returned to the front and my breath caught in my throat. That singular moment in my life; remembered now so many years later, as clear as if it was this morning. The coursing of an emotion I had never felt before but would feel many times after. Intense, burning, fearfully encompassing shame.

The young men had been tethered to the white poles. Their heads down, their shoulders slumped. An old man in a long flowing robe stepped forward from the VIP seating area. He carried a book and stopped at each of the men in turn. His words were inaudible to me, yet it seemed that as each conversation ended the younger man held his head higher, stood straighter, ignored his bindings. I remember wondering about that. But I didn't dwell on it. Not then.

A boy of about my age asked his father, too loudly in my opinion, what the men were called.

'Targets.' The father laughed and some of the other men and women around them joined in. 'May pole dancers.'

I didn't understand the jokes, but I felt sick in the pit of my stomach at their laughter. Movement in the square brought a renewed hush. The Welsh driver had come back into the middle. He placed a hood over each of the young men's heads before marching smartly away. The dozen soldiers in their two lines came to attention, their soft soles making little noise. No yelled commands, no parade ground stamping. Just quiet efficiency. They moved like twelve puppets with shared strings. Then they stood, rock-solid. Still.

A women officer stepped from the bus and checked her watch. She nodded almost imperceptibly and the forward row of six soldiers knelt down whilst the rear row took half a pace forward. All swung their rifles up into their shoulders and aimed them forward. Silence, so achingly intrusive, descended again. I know I had stopped breathing. I think the rest of that huge crowd had too.

The first notes of Westminster Quarters sounded across the London skyline. Rhythmic, gentle, echoing sadly in my ears. I have never heard them since without being taken to that time, that day. Then the pause, that small, insignificant pause. Not normally registered, acknowledged or understood. But I understood it then. I willed it not to end and I failed. The deep resonant tone of the thirteen ton bell sounded and on that first stroke to mark the sixth hour, twelve rifles fired in unison. Their sharp report scoured the square. Pigeons fluttered up, flying to escape the jarring, shattering violence. Yet I could not fly and so I stood with the rest of the watching crowd as four lives were torn apart. I blinked back tears and struggled to hold down the feelings of regret that threatened to have me vomit. I looked away and then, with a resilience I didn't know I had, forced myself to look back.

Their bodies hung in limp surrender to gravity, held upright only by their wrists tied to the posts. Dark blood pumped onto the ground and formed deep purple pools in the sand. The earth bank behind was gaudily covered in splashes of vibrant red.

My dad turned to me and nodded in mute recognition of my emotions. Then we went home on the Tube. That was London, May Day Holiday 2050. A quarter of a century ago. The weekly executions. I asked my dad why we did it.

'There's a war on boy. We fight fire with fire.'

I gazed up at him, 'Won't that just mean we all burn?'

Ian Andrew

Pumpkin Punch

Clive stood in the corner of the dining room. He let out a long despondent sigh. His beautiful mahogany table, that he'd had custom made by a bespoke carpenter in Cornwall, was covered with a garish Halloween themed tablecloth. It was bright orange and dotted with black cats, bats and broomsticks. There were a whole manner of scary items dangling from the ceiling on varying lengths of cotton. Big globs of blue tac held them in place. *That'll stain the ceiling*, he thought. Large ornate candles were everywhere, their flame lost in the brightness of the room. They gave off a sweet sickly smell like an old man's breath after sucking on a Werther's Original. They were nothing like the *Scent of Scary Pumpkin* that had been advertised.

The room was humming with the mundane conversations of the twelve or so guests. There was a large crystal punchbowl in the centre of the table. It had dulled with age and looked like it had come straight from a charity shop. It was filled with luminous green liquid that looked like snot, *tasted like it too*, Clive would remark later. About six fake eyeballs bobbed lazily around in the putrid looking gloop. *Tasteful—real tasteful!*

There was a plate of sausages that had been made to look like severed fingers. He examined one closely, was about to put it in his mouth, but the cold dead skin feel of them put him right off. He placed it back on the plate.

Gloria gushed into the dining room with all the presence

and theatrics of a semi-professional drag queen. Clive raised his eyebrows in exasperation. Her face was painted green, but it was too bright. She looked more like a Granny Smith apple than a Wicked Witch. She had a witch's hat perched on her head. The strap dug in and gave the impression of a double chin. She wore a black bed sheet that was supposed to look like a cape. It looked like a bed sheet. Clive shook his head in quiet disdain. He could hear her warbling like a magpie as she flitted from guest to guest.

'Cliiiiive,' she purred as she approached him. 'Stop being a party pooper, come and mingle.'

Her hand emerged from her bedsheet and ruffled his hair. His jaw clenched in quiet controlled anger. She gave him a peck on the lips. Her breath smelt of eggs. He got a taste of her face paint for good measure, it tasted like chalk and reminded him of school. Her top lip was sweating, and the paint was running. *Yuk.*

'I'm just popping out for some air; I'll be back soon enough to play the congenial host,' Clive replied without any hint of sarcasm… *that was hard.*

He grabbed a boiled sweet from a large plastic bowl, popped it into his mouth and made his way outside. He spat the boiled sweet into the hedgerow, it was an aniseed ball and tasted like a toilet cube!

He walked out onto his south London street. The October air was ice cold and had a menthol effect when he took a deep breath in. It felt good.

Groups of small children were milling about, faces filled with greedy anticipation of the treats they were going to get. A small boy dressed as Woody from Toy Story approached him.

'Trick or treat mate,' he chirped expectantly.

'Piss of ya little beggar,' Clive replied with not a hint of humour.

The boy's look of hope immediately faded into one of disappointment. He turned and ran back to his friends. The boy pointed towards Clive; all the other lads looked over at the same time.

'Fuck you, ya tight arsehole!' One of the older kids shouted over, causing raucous cackling from the rest of the bunch. They all ran off at high speed, their laughter disappearing with them into the night.

'Fucking degenerates!' Clive shouted after them.

He turned to go back into the house and was met with a shrill scream. This was not a fake Halloween scream. Something was wrong—very very wrong!

Clive was met by complete pandemonium when he rushed into the dining room. Gloria was laying on her side. Her chest was heaving and hitching trying to draw in breath but failing. Her eyes were bulging in their sockets, a look of sublime fear in her eyes. The noise of her struggle was hideous; she sounded like a pig being slaughtered. Betty from number twenty-two was frantically dialling the emergency services on her phone. Her husband Ted was kneeling next to Gloria.

'I ain't doing no CPR on 'er, she's got puke in 'er mouth,' Ted moaned

'Yeah, she'll do the same for you one day dickhead—get outta my fucking way!'

Clive shoved Ted to one side, sat Gloria up and with one arm across her ample bosom he slapped her hard and firm in the middle of her shoulder blades. He would admit later that the first aid course his company had insisted he attended was finally good for something. On the third hard blow of her back, Gloria gurgled, coughed twice, and expelled a green slimy mass from her mouth. She drew in deep, whiney life-giving breaths. Betty from number twenty-two fainted.

'Oh my Gawd…. Oh My Gawd!' Gloria wheezed.

'Deep breaths doll, deep breaths,' Clive soothed.

Ted pulled a handkerchief out of his shirt pocket and picked the small round object covered in green gloop up from the floor. It was a fake eyeball. Clive plucked it from Ted's hand and looked at it with disdain. Ted scurried off to attend to Betty who had her hand on her forehead and was swooning herself back to consciousness.

Clive turned to his wife. 'Crap party honey… But by fuck—the punch was to die for! Party's over folks.'

Mark Townsend

About the Bunbury Writers Group

Founded in 2018 BWG is a small and intimate group of local writers who meet fortnightly to share, read and critique each others work.

If you are interested in coming to a meeting, then drop us a line at our email, bunburywritersgroup@gmail.com. Also come and follow us on our Facebook page 'Bunbury Writers Group' or on our Instagram account, bunbury_writers_group.

Or simply come along to one of our regular meetings held in the marvellous Caf-fez, 18-20 Prinsep St, Bunbury WA 6230.

If you would like to know about any of the authors featured in the book, full biographies can be found at,

https://bookreality.com/project/bunbury-writers-group

Acknowledgments

We would like to acknowledge the following people, without whom this book could not have been produced:

Lisa Townsend for her amazing cover design. To Oliver Townsend for the additional graphic work. To the City of Bunbury for their generous funding of local community and art groups and finally, heartfelt thanks to Caf-Fez for giving us space to meet in a place that is never disenchanted.